W9-BWD-345

translated from the French by

Sheila Fischman

Viking
Published by the Penguin Group
Penguin Books Canada Ltd, 10 Alcorn Avenue, Toronto, Ontario, Canada M4V 3B2
Penguin Books Ltd, 27 Wrights Lane, London W8 5TZ, England
Viking Penguin, a division of Penguin Books USA Inc., 375 Hudson Street, New York, New York 10014, U.S.A.
Penguin Books Australia Ltd, Ringwood, Victoria, Australia
Penguin Books (NZ) Ltd, 182-190 Wairau Road, Auckland 10, New Zealand

Penguin Books Ltd, Registered Offices: Harmondsworth, Middlesex, England

First published 1994

10 9 8 7 6 5 4 3 2 1

Printed and bound in Canada on acid free paper ♾

Canadian Cataloguing in Publication Data

Carrier, Roch, 1937-
[Fin. English]
The end

Translation of: Fin.
ISBN 0-670-85454-9

I. Title. II. Title: Fin. English.

PQ8505.A7752F5513 1994 C843'.54 C93-094942-0
PQ3919.2.C37F5513 1994

the end

the end

What must happen has become inevitable. My dears, I would like to tell you why Victor Joyeux has to leave us. You know who is speaking to you through the voice of the notary, but I still have to say my name. That is how a will begins.

I may as well describe to you at the outset, my dears, the most beautiful moment in my life. Just in case I forget—in case I should decide to interrupt this will... It was not the first time I made love, nor when I saw the Taj Mahal, nor when I kissed the rock of the Calvary in Jerusalem, nor the time the young actress took off her brassiere when we were taking the elevator up to my hotel suite, nor when the Prime Minister invited me to a private lunch, nor my first flight over the Rocky Mountains, nor when I got my green electric train, my first bicycle, my first car. The only time that I'd still like to remember when I'm on the other side, as my mother used to say, on the other side of life...

Why can't I remember what island we were on? I see very clearly the palm trees, the huts, the beach and the road between the sea and our villa. I remember the long verandah and the maid. Where was it? It was an island in the sun, as they say. My daughter, Christiana, had captured a fish in the little hole she'd dug in the sand to imprison the sea, as she put it. The fish had got stuck in the hole and Christiana decided to keep it. She brought it up to the house in her red bucket. The poor fish survived both being alone and being overfed. Christiana shared with it everything she ate. The fish refused nothing. Every day, Christiana, wearing her pink bikini and all the seriousness of a three-year-old, replenished the water for her fish, whose name, we had learned, was Edmond.

Edmond in his bucket became the most important member of the family, the one she spent most of her time with. She even neglected her teddy bear. She would sing her fish to sleep. She would tell him stories in a language no one else could understand. Thanks to Edmond, our family had never been more united!

And then we had to leave the island—where was it? Our holidays were over. Christiana wanted to take her fish home. She asked me to reserve a seat beside her for the fish. She'd packed a travelling bag for it, with some pebbles, a bottle of sand and one of water, seaweed, cookies and a jar of vitamin pills. When he was as big as Christiana he'd be able to go to her school! In fact, she had sent her kindergarten principal a postcard that both she and Edmond had signed. The name of Leonardo da Vinci will be erased from my memory before Edmond's.

I didn't want any trouble at customs. Edmond could have caused some. A customs officer, bald on his head and hairy inside, a prisoner in his booth and as jealous as a legless person watching a marathon, might have read in his big book of things forbidden that Edmond could not immigrate into Canada. What a tragedy that would be! I wanted to protect Christiana from human mediocrity. I didn't want her to hate her country because some customs officer had forced a little girl to part from her summer friend.

I undertook to convince Christiana that Edmond would be lonely in Canada. It would be better to leave him at home, in his own country.

"What would you think, Christiana, if someone took you away to a country you didn't know? Canada is much too cold for Edmond. He doesn't have boots or a fur coat. He can't go skiing or snowshoeing. If you were a fish like Edmond, how would you like to be taken away from the sea?"

Christiana replied:

"I'm going to take Edmond back now to his house by the rock."

During that summer I too had grown rather attached to Edmond. I'd often gone to the sea to fetch cool water for him. He had given Christiana so much happiness: I could only love him. With everything Christiana had told him about me and what she'd told me about him, Edmond and I were almost friends. I too had, as the children say, a sad heart.

Carrying Edmond in his red bucket, Christiana started down the road to the sea. I waved like someone bidding farewell to a friend...Edmond!

All at once, she stopped. She turned around. She noticed me watching her. She was coming back towards me. I was terror-stricken; had Christiana decided to go back home with Edmond? I decided that I'd use my paternal strength to return the damned fish to the place he should never have left. To my engineer's mind it seemed absolutely irrational to import that fish to Canada, where the oceans are overpopulated with other fish that are just as insignificant as Edmond.

"Papa, I want you to come and help me in case Edmond's forgotten how to swim in the sea."

What an idiot I'd been, with my engineer's head! A tear came to my eye. It was as salty as the entire sea. I held out my hand to my daughter and she grasped it. Now she felt very strong. She had the strength she was attributing to her father. Little girl, will you ever know that when he held your little hand in his he felt imbued with the power of the mystery that creates life and conquers time? I was no longer a man who was walking towards the sea, but a god who was continuing the creation of the world.

Christiana dropped Edmond into the water.

"He doesn't want to go, Papa."

Edmond was peacefully swimming in circles, showing little curiosity about the sea.

"He's afraid because there's too much water around him," Christiana explained.

An excellent opportunity for some fatherly pontificating.

"Most of the time we're afraid when we feel too small in this life."

"Papa, he doesn't want to leave us."

"Very well, we'll stay with him for a while. In his new life he'll become a great navigator and travel around the world."

(After I've put an end to my days will someone accompany me to help me in my new life? I shouldn't even think about that. Alone I came, and naked. I am clothed now for my departure, but still alone.)

Several years later... Somewhere a pickpocket makes off with your years, you don't feel his hand but you suddenly no longer have those bills from the great bank of time. They've flown away. Some years later, I was on an island—was it in the Marquesas? I was going to walk in the water; I like the gritty softness of sand, and the terrible softness of the water. Your feet seem like someone else's, the sand seems as far from you as the depths of the sky. You feel that you're no longer altogether on the Earth.

That time in the Marquesas—or was it Tahiti?—there was a fish, always the same one, following me: a fish the size of my pen, which the islanders call (in my translation) silver belly. Every time I went into the water, Silver Belly was there, swimming single-mindedly. All at once I had the feeling it was Edmond, the fish Christiana had tamed.

It was not Edmond, of course. It's an insane story I've never told before. That insignificant animal with his dumb eyes had no memory. Edmond was so unintelligent, he must have been eaten long ago. Deep down, however, a sort of conviction that was beyond my control assured me that it could be Edmond. Such a fantasy is not the product of an engineer's mind. It's something Christiana could have invented and believed in at the age of three... To recognize Edmond the fish some years later, in another sea... I'm a reasonable man, but fantasies often break away from my reason like young calves from a pen.

When my eyes are closed for the Great Sleep—logically, the Great Sleep that comes after life should resemble the Great Sleep that precedes it—perhaps then I'll have the privilege of dreaming. Did I dream before my birth? The night, I believe, was smooth, blue, dreamless. I was born with a memory filled with forgotten dreams! Should I dream after my life, then, I would like those dreams to be about my daughter going down to the beach to return her fish to the sea.

I am an engineer and I'm not very fond of words. Numbers are better at expressing my thoughts. Pre-stressed concrete hasn't inspired very many poets. It is a mass, a power, an immobility that has no need of words to help it endure. It is a rock, without the beauty of rock.

So many words to explain that I barely use words. Since I began this last will and testament, words have been getting away from me like wasps from a nest that's been shaken. That's just what I am doing: before I set out on the Great Crossing, I'm shaking up my memory a little.

I'm amazed to see myself using so many words. Before, in twenty-five words I could sum up a problem, offer a solution, or describe the entire world. And even then I considered myself too effusive. Here I am, victim of a tornado of words, a flood of adjectives, a landslide of syntax, an earthquake of metaphors, a volcanic eruption of verbs. If I don't stop, I'll be late for carrying out the plan that is going to propel me into Absolute Silence.

Soon I shall be silent. Is that what is compelling me to write so much? My brain, operating at top speed, is restlessly rushing in a verbal stampede. My hand is tracing signs that will dry like leaves that fall though the tree still lives. Is it my way of crying out before I rush into the Great Ignorance? I don't want to cry out. The edge of the cliff doesn't frighten me... All this writing is showing me that I can write poetry again.

I had left the city with its traffic jams, its noise, its distractions, its exponential acceleration... The city is a particle accelerator. Just then, everything was moving too quickly for someone who was trying to explore his soul, his memory, his imagination, like the planets in a galaxy. Instead of getting lost in ourselves, I thought, we are losing ourselves in the electrical labyrinth of the streets. Did you know that, my dears? Before I became an engineer in pre-stressed concrete, I was a poet. I left the city for an island where one could hear the sea in dialogue with the land.

Unfathomable mystery of the sky! Poetry of life!

There is another memory that I wouldn't want to leave behind me. A muslin curtain stirs, and I am happy. I'm happy because the curtain is moving. The breeze that swells it touches me as well. I'm as happy to feel it as if it were the robe of an invisible angel. I feel the angel's breath on my face. Hearing it makes me happy. It utters no words, but communicates through thought, as our teacher explained to us. Undoubtedly it is speaking to me from Heaven because I am filled with a great and luminous happiness. My mother had decided not to send me to school. That morning I'd been suffering from a stomach ache, but then the pain let up. I'm happy that I'm not at school, that I'm at home in this bedroom which is only opened up when aunts and uncles come to visit. I'm happy to be liberated from school, to hear my mother humming. I'm happy to see the light behind the muslin that is swelling like the water in a lake as it becomes a wave. I am happy to see the light, the breeze and the muslin all play together.

And here I am, my dears, I, the engineer in pre-stressed concrete, concrete reinforced with taut steel cables, concrete that imitates granite, here I am, I, engineer of the hard, the solid, the motionless, lingering over a description of a moving curtain. At this moment as I'm about to undertake the Great Voyage, I am concerned about remembering not my bridges, my dams or my buildings, but a fluttering curtain. That curtain is something I haven't forgotten. I'd like to see it again after I've departed this planet. I don't remember much about myself when I was a child in my bed in pajamas, instead of being at school. I hope that image of a curtain in which the breeze is creating waves will not grow dim.

At times when I was sad, at times when I was happy, at times when I was alone or in good company, at times when I was here, and at other times when I was pacing far-off valleys of the Earth, I saw again that muslin curtain at the window of the bedroom that was only opened for uncles and aunts who had come from far away or for children when they had a fever. Like the wings of a very big bird, it soared above me. I remembered then that happiness on this planet does exist. Once I've run away from it, I would like the great bird of sun-drenched muslin to remind me again that happiness on earth once existed.

Everything will be simple. I'm going to drive my car into the viaduct. At a hundred and fifty kilometres an hour the margin of error is virtually non-existent. I will succeed. When the speedometer shows one hundred and forty, I shall unfasten my seat-belt. I'll have already unscrewed the caps on the cans of gas. On impact the cans will overturn. I can't fail. Those who bungle their departures are those who organize their deaths as badly as their lives. But what the hell, it takes planning. You don't fling yourself into the unknown with your eyes closed. It takes calculation. Most people are afraid to add up one and one. In my case, I've calculated as an engineer does. I no longer know if I enjoyed my profession, but at least it has let me know the precise space that I occupy in life, instead of floating limply like ectoplasm in an opaque liquid. I've chosen the perfect spot for the Great Conclusion, a viaduct under the highway. It's solid and I know it very well: I built it. The Roads Department is surprised that it's already peeling and crumbling, that the cables are rusting. One day, perhaps, officials will understand that our northern climate is different from that at the Equator. And their budgets should reflect that difference.

We always look for motives, secret reasons, when a person puts an end to his days, as we say.

The legend will surely be told of the concrete engineer who hurled himself into one of his own structures: the work that destroys its maker.

When I'm almost at the viaduct, I'll just have to turn my wheel slightly to the left, then I'll veer off and drive into the pillar of the viaduct. One corner of it will ram the radiator grille like a knife sinking into butter.

The world is full of irony. In the very place where a sign proclaims "Maximum speed 90," I'm going to step on the gas! Before that, I'll have stopped to make the final preparations. The shoulder must be level: I don't want the gasoline cans to overturn before the fateful moment. I'd hate to be burned alive. It must be horribly painful. If I fear anything it's not death, but suffering. And so at that point I will unscrew the caps on the gas cans. Then I'll spray gasoline on my clothes, using a little atomizer. I've replaced the perfume in it with gasoline. Then I'll get into the car, fasten my seat-belt, roll up the windows, turn off the air-conditioning and get into gear for my final journey. I'm going to accelerate as planned. When I reach the clump of poplars, I'll use the car lighter to light a cigarette.

At that point everything could explode, but it would be too soon. I must be prudent. I'll be as cautious as the Chinese who transported the nitro-glycerine when they were digging the railway tunnels through the Rockies. If I'm cautious, I'll be able to avoid an explosion. And so I unfasten my seat-belt, my left hand is on the wheel—it's easy because the road is straight—and I accelerate. With my right hand I press the lighter, then I pick up the cigarette that's waiting in the ashtray; after the click, I shall light it. No sparks, because there's no air circulating. I bring it to my lips, I accelerate again. Now I'm very close to the viaduct, I turn the wheel a little to the left. My car is flattened against my viaduct. Starting there, I set out on my Great Vacation. The lighted cigarette has fallen from my lips, rolled onto my gasoline-soaked clothes. With the shock, the cans have overturned, the car bursts like a bomb and writhes in the black smoke. That's what you call going out with a bang! It will be the end. At that moment, everything that can be calculated will be finished.

At that precise moment, Victor Joyeux will cease to be alive. Or will he perhaps remain alive in some other way? I'll see, I'll know. At that moment I shall be like Edmond, Christiana's fish, thrown from my little bucket back into the sea. I'll start to swim in the unknown of my new life, my new universe, my new dimension, my new time, my new country, my new non-existence.

What is this gibberish? Why this need to philosophize? Even when I was living on my island writing poems, I had a visceral hatred of verbiage: the same hatred that I confess I feel for those who waste life's precious moments.

Everything must be and will be precise. Over and over I've reviewed the procedure for my Permanent Retreat. I've inspected both the highway and the viaduct. My cigarette will be of crucial importance. According to my calculations, I'll be smashed like a wild strawberry under the hoof of a rutting bull. Still, two precautions are better than one. The explosion will provide me with a second protection, I would say: If for some unforeseeable, non-mathematical reason the collision does not achieve its goal, then fire will succeed where concrete failed.

You know, my dears, about that ceremony in India in which the body of the dead, lying on a pyre, is put to the torch. After spending a lifetime trying to put together a few certainties, to follow solid principles, to build some permanent things, my life is going to be turned into smoke. In a sense, fire will reveal what I have never ceased to be: smoke.

the end

I must be precise. The cigarette is important and, like many important things, it is also small and insignificant. Everything must be anticipated. I haven't smoked a cigarette since I was young. It would be tragic if it should go out because I had forgotten how to inhale. It would be tragic if I started to cough: there would be a risk of premature sparks on my clothes. To avoid risks I'll need to have absolute control over the act of smoking. The best way to ensure that was to start smoking again. The fashion of the day dictates that we must stop smoking. It's another of those instances of mass hysteria that succeed one another in the history of a society perpetually but superficially seeking the cause of all the ills it is prey to. I've gone back to smoking. My astonished friends have accused me of succumbing to a vice.

"If smoking were a vice," I told them, "I'd never have stopped and I'd be smoking twice as much now."

"By smoking you're inflicting lung cancer on yourself."

"I'm a suicidal type," I declared. My friends laughed.

I apply myself to smoking with a certain pleasure. I want to succeed at this project which is undoubtedly more important for me than for you; more important too than all my stadiums, bridges, viaducts and other weighty, poor-quality constructions. Great actors prepare for their entrances on stage. I must prepare for mine even more assiduously, I who am not an actor.

Can it be that I've already left the planet? Is the little explosion I'm preparing a mere ritual to make official a departure that has already taken place?

Yesterday, the city was jubilant. The radio was announcing: "Join us in mass intoxication: drink our beer." Or: "We're as happy as pigs; let's drink like pigs!"

Don't ask me why, but I found myself in a big procession. I was drawn to it. By the radio? The newspaper? Has my life become so empty that I was expecting to find something there? Was it nostalgia for that great day every year when the People celebrates its joy and pride in being the People? I've always found nationalist demonstrations as boring as Mass. I've never had any sympathy for that shouting by a People who stupidly—in the same way they pay taxes, the same way they vote—repeat the slogans of some clever group or other. The People like simple solutions.

I went to the demonstration with Melissa. Melissa is twenty. Children, when they're normal, enjoy such gatherings. She didn't believe that I could be so young.

"You old wolf, most men your age only want their slippers, but here you are about to demonstrate on behalf of the People!"

Ah, how happy she was! I said to her:

"My eighty-six-year-old mother is going to take part in the local celebrations in her neighbourhood."

Melissa was dancing with admiration.

"Your family is eternal, you old wolf!"

"Eternal!"

ETERNAL? Perhaps.

She was beautiful in her oversized T-shirt with her little breasts standing out beneath the blue slogan: *One Land for our People, One People for our Land*. I took her hand. It was forbidden fruit in the hand of a sixty-one-year-old man.

The People had come here to this main thoroughfare to trample each other's toes and to shove each other around. There were bugles, drums, xylophones, an accordion; their music blended together and became noise. There were shouts, banners, flags. Arms were raised in the air. I've noticed that at these demonstrations they use only one arm. What do they do with the other? And what was I doing there?

The crowd stood still. They marched. They yelled. They fell silent. The sun was beating down. Flags were waved. They were squeezed together, shoulder to shoulder, chest to chest. Everyone was sweating. Everyone smelled the way you might expect. And the People, unanimously—as a much-applauded political hack declared—demanded to be *the* People. What was I doing there?

The People, I thought, are clumsily demanding the correction of what they clumsily perceive as a slight. The cries of the crowd came together in a roar as powerful as the rumbling of the sea on those days when it deploys almost all of its mighty force. And I thought: That crowd is a great wounded beast. Or is the beast angry? I remained silent. I could not cry like those on all sides of me. With one arm around Melissa's shoulders, pushed along by the crowd, and enjoying the warmth of her body, I held her against me very tightly. She had stopped shouting her slogan. I tried to make a joke:

"Put a little more conviction in your protest, child!"

She turned her beautiful green eyes towards

me. Her eyes were filled with tears that overflowed onto her beautiful cheeks that were made for kisses. She told me:

"Thank you, old wolf, for letting me witness the victory of a people!"

I was no longer really present at the demonstration; for some time now I'd been elsewhere. Though I was walking in a crowd of one hundred and fifty thousand, I wasn't with them.

Melissa: I love that young beauty who gives herself to me as if I were the good Lord Himself. Youth and age do not repel one another, but neither can you add them up or calculate the average. I can share things with Melissa's mother, as she does with me. Her mother has lived, I have lived: each of us is curious about the other. Youth has generosity, but not much curiosity. With Melissa, there is no exchange: I take her youth, which she gives me. At twenty we like to give ourselves. I love her. I love her the way we love going back to our own adolescence. I love her like a beautiful memory of adolescence. Loving Melissa is like rereading a novel you first read at fifteen. Loving Melissa is knowing that youth has not altogether deserted me. It is realizing that youth is not afraid of age. Loving Melissa is looking at myself in a mirror that loves me. Loving

Melissa is escaping from the ghetto of age. It means learning that life is not over. Loving Melissa is starting life over, in the same way we like to watch a videotape again. Loving Melissa means being loved.

If anyone cries at my funeral it will be Melissa. How she will cry! My dears, choose the church closest to the river for the ceremony, for you'll have to collect her tears. Oh Melissa, it's not worth feeling all that sorrow. Seeing you dressed all in black and filled with so much sorrow, a handsome young cousin of your age who has come to bury me will feel it is his duty to console you.

Since I started writing this last will and testament, I've used more words than I've used in my whole life. I only wanted to put down the name of the trust company that's going to administer and distribute my possessions. This will is becoming as thick as the Bible.

Here I am then, in full regression, back to the days when I was writing my poems. That was when I preferred my ten words lined up on a white page to a steak with green peppercorns. Those days are far behind me now. There are too many words in the world. Life is covered with a dust of words. Life is flooded with words. To achieve the essential reality—ah, my vocabulary is as stiff as my legs are in the morning—to touch real life, one must dig beneath linguistic sediment. Too many words. And here I am adding to them. I'm contributing to the plague of verbal locusts that devour the leaves, the flowers, the fruits of real life. Gripped by a sudden frenzy, I'm producing a proliferation of words. Is it because I am on my way to the Great Silence?

No one will read this will. It will be on the front seat beside me when I plunge into the Great Void. It won't explain my flight. I have nothing to explain. No one really needs me to explain. No one would really listen if I did explain. No one would understand. I don't understand myself. I shall do what I must do. Quite simply. Does the seed understand how it becomes a flower? Does the tree understand how it shrivels and dies? Does the stream understand how it turns to ice under the sharp light of December? Does the ice understand how it becomes water again? Does the Earth understand why it turns? Life makes, life becomes. I make, I become. I don't understand, I don't explain. I can proclaim, however—I, an engineer in pre-stressed concrete—that I am tired of things that are heavy, rigid, solid and durable.

23

It's been more than twenty years since I've eaten a rare steak. I like my meat rare. God did not create well-done meat. For a long time now I've been avoiding red meat and sauces. I was afraid of cholesterol. I wanted to keep my arteries clear so the blood could circulate. I was right. I've stayed alive. It's idiotic to die because you've eaten too much sauce. Before I take flight, I'm going to indulge in a thick and tender steak with green peppercorn sauce. I must make a note in my daybook. At an intimate dinner with Melissa... No, that would be a mistake! She's too young to relish what she eats. With her mother then. Just the two of us, a dinner by candlelight. A secluded corner. Melissa's mother, my leg touching hers under the table. She knows that youth departs. Melissa thinks it will last forever. Melissa is completely taken up with being young. Melissa and her mother are the same woman: I meet one in the morning when the light is new, the other is with me at the end of the day when I ask myself what the day was made of.

At the patriotic demonstration where the flags beat their wings and the marchers were cackling, Melissa suddenly wrenched herself away from my arm—at her age her mother probably had the same waist—and her hip was quivering.

the end

She had spotted a group of friends: their placards demanded that the province become a country. I said to Melissa:

"If the province breaks away from the country, why shouldn't the city break away from the province? Why shouldn't my neighbourhood break away from the city? Why shouldn't my street break away from the neighbourhood? And why shouldn't my property break away from my street? I can easily picture my flag floating over my house, above my independent garden. Do you know what I'd choose as a national emblem? Your little buttocks, Melissa." I thought: I'll tell your mother they're hers.

Melissa replied, in the curt tone of those who are no longer altogether young:

"Victor, it's our world now, not yours... I'm going to join them. We're all at university together. Se-pa-ra-tion! Se-pa-ra-tion!"

She was already chanting the slogans along with them. At my age you don't separate, you don't divide any more. After travelling so many roads, I've come to this hill from where we can see that everything is united, everything has assembled, that everything holds together. We are cells that move, that devour one another, that die and are reborn in a great moving sea that is indifferent to both separations and unions. I see no difference between the sea that rises up to send a powerful wave against a rocky cliff and the heart in a person's chest that emits a code to push death away for a while.

When Melissa left me to join her group of friends I had tears in my eyes. All at once youth was breaking away from me. Now I was alone with my age. I'll have tears in my eyes again when I drive my car into that viaduct I built fourteen or fifteen years ago. Will I think about you then, Melissa? Will I think about your mother? Will I think of that child—was it in Costa Rica or in Panama?—who brought a platter of fruit to my room in the morning? Will I think of other lady friends with whom I've lived a few moments of eternity along the roads of this world? I cannot forget them. Will I think of one of my grandchildren who, driving a little car I gave him, will also in his way collide with the viaduct of the real world? Good luck, child! I'd be pleased if, amid my tears, those were my final words.

Melissa and her friends want to separate the province from the country. They believe that will make their lives better. I have reached the age at which one is convinced there is no separation possible. Springing from the same source, going towards a common destination, it's quite possible that everything that exists has a common skin, as one of my poets said, a common blood.

With their slogans and their flags, Melissa and her friends think of themselves as great magicians. For thousands of years, humans have been coupling. Melissa and her friends have discovered that humankind needs a sexual revolution. Melissa made me go to see that singer, the pudgy one with legs like a donkey's, who dances. The singer says that making love should be as simple as walking down the street. A dick is made of the same flesh as a nose. Making love in public should be no more forbidden than smiling. In that way, the old bourgeois hypocrisy would be killed. In that way a sexual taboo that, according to the singer, is firmly planted like a very tall totem pole above society would be brought down. I with my old morality, my prejudices and my thousand-odd women, I declare: If the charter of human rights guarantees me the right to exhibit my dick along the boulevards, does that give a slice of bread to the children in countries struck by famine?

Before I bury myself in the Great Darkness, I think of the millions who are starving to death, I think of the millions with no water to drink. I think of the millions of persons who are pushed, along with stones and garbage, by the blades of bulldozers as they make room for new cities. I think of the millions of persons gnawed at by the vermin of superstition. I think of the wars that teach us that animals are less cruel than the one species that believes in God. I think of the thousands for whom life is suffering and who reproduce themselves, perpetuating that suffering. I think of the millions who hope for reincarnation as an animal that is less unhappy than a human being. Such desperate souls I've seen everywhere: in Brazil, where the street children will never be human again; in India, in Sierra Leone, in Bangladesh, in Pakistan, in New York and even in this fine provincial town of ours. Melissa, can your singer's little sexual revolution help those millions wounded by life? Will the separation of the province bring them something to eat?

Melissa, and you, her young friends, listen: For those wretched of the Earth, your provincial nationalism, your sexual revolution, are fantasies of the rich. It is through union, cooperation, trust, friendship that the unfortunate will be given some relief. And that, Melissa, is why there were tears in my eyes when I watched you marching under those nationalist banners. We have just one life, Melissa, and we're squandering it on so many pointless actions.

If I were logical, I would use an airplane for my Great Flight, use the broad wings of my little Cessna to climb, higher, higher, until my eardrums buzz, higher still, *altius*, climb until they burst, climb until the azure sky smashes the aircraft and tears it like a sheet of paper, then descends, descends towards that land from which no one returns.

Often, in my sleep, I've heard a *bang* that woke me up. I know now, that *bang* is the shock of my Jaguar against the viaduct. I've sometimes heard it even when I wasn't asleep. During the daytime. At the office. When I was bent over my plans. *Bang!* It woke me up, in a sense. Could it be that life is sleep? Could it be that I will only be awake on the other side of the viaduct? It's the former versifier who is dreaming like this. For the moment, though, let us accept no illusions. No lies. No poetry. Let us seek the weighty truth of the concrete of reality. Many times my nocturnal companions have been wakened by my cry. "It was a nightmare," I'd explain. I never confessed to my loves that I'd heard a loud *bang* because I had slammed into something very hard. Was that nightmare *bang* announcing, already, the final Big Bang? It's the old failed poet in me who whispers that supposition. Could it be that the *bang* that resounded in my sleep when I was just a child is the recollection, imprinted in the memory of minerals, plants and animals, of that first explosion, that first birth, when the Mother of the World cast from her womb the first spark of life?

This dream doesn't hold much meaning for the engineer I've become, but it fascinates the poet I never let myself be, who is reawakening today. Before life is erased he demands to write what he has never expressed. Does that old poet who has never really lived want to give some meaning to the life of the engineer who has lived too much? What does that mean, to live too much? To live? A few women. Some travelling. Some big objects made of pre-stressed concrete. A few dreams. A few nightmares. Is that living too much? Is it living?

To climb on board a Cessna and let myself drop? No thanks. I need security in the exercise of life as much as in that of death… I will not write that word. I don't like it. Lots of people come out of a plane crash alive. I have to put every chance on my side, leave nothing to destiny: the pre-stressed concrete viaduct, the charging car, the cans of gasoline, the lit cigarette. Those are my guarantees of success. By calculating everything, I don't think I'll survive long enough to be aware of the noise of the explosion. I hope, though, that I'll be able to register the vertigo of my flight. I shall be scattered in smoke above the suburbs. Some of my cells may live on in the fire, like salamanders in the ashes of my bones, which will crackle and burn like splinters of dry wood. I hope I will taste the stunning giddiness of taking flight, of escaping gravity, of rising up free of my carcass and my cubic tons of pre-stressed concrete. I've never been able to escape the recurring sensation that someone had cast a net over me that was enclosing me, surrounding me, that was weighing on my body, on my movements, my ideas, my emotions and my dreams. Heritage, culture, education, religion, politics, routine, discomforts—on Wednesday I'll shatter that mould! I have been a submissive man. I've lived like a caterpillar in its cocoon. Wednesday will be the day of the butterfly!

Now is not the time for weeping. I who have never talked about myself am listening to written words with so much pleasure! I've turned off the record player. To hell with Mozart! The pre-stressed concrete engineer is taking the floor to declare his independence on the Wednesday of the Great Escape. I'm short and bald and round in the belly, but I shall be free!

Concrete, to hell with you. I've abdicated in favour of pre-stressed concrete and it—make no mistake—never hesitates. Concrete doesn't need to talk. It exists. And through it I, too, once existed. Words were very slight compared with concrete. Words were only the shadow of reality. I've gradually renounced my ideas, my feelings. My soul has been closed up for years, the way you close up a cottage for the winter.

Never has a last will and testament been so long. This is the point at which my lawyer should tell my heirs they can take a break to go answer nature's call.

I am hungry for things that are light. Looking up at the sky the other day I saw a shark, a green shark with a smile. A balloon that some children were flying. I watched them let out the string and free the green shark, then haul it in. They were as captivated by it as some old fishermen gone to sea.

I was fascinated. One of the children offered me the string.

"Play with it, make it tired."

The shark stirred and climbed to swim a

little higher. It made me happier than I'd been in a long time. I told the children:

"I'd like to buy your green shark. How much?"

A little boy replied:

"We can't sell it to you, you aren't a kid."

On Wednesday, the day of the Great Explosion, I'm going to let go of the string. And I, the green shark, will climb.

Wednesday. In three days I shall claim my independence from life. Melissa wants independence for her province. The water is polluted. Drinkable water is rarer than petroleum. The fish are sick. The forests are dying. The birds are poisoned. The nuclear reactors are packing it in. We bury waste the way we hide the truth. Children have learned nothing but violence. Peace is becoming more violent than war. What independent country can resolve these problems? What independent country can stop pollution, violence or despair from crossing borders? Who will kill that stupid old idea of the dinosaurs?:

> "This territory belongs to me, I mark it with my urine and because my muzzle is stronger than yours, you must not step onto my territory, and if you do, you must

33

recognize that my urine is the best urine in the world and you must swear an oath to fight and die for my urine on this territory."

The Earth that flies in space resembles, I can see it today, the Raft of the Medusa. In my opinion, too much light and clouds are spattered across that painting, and the victims of the wreck, who had starved for weeks, who had fought and torn one another apart, are shown with oily torsos like those you see on the covers of magazines for muscle-bound exhibitionists. I'm more interested in the story behind the painting, for the fate of those hundred and fifty victims is also the history of humankind. They were five hundred at the beginning of the adventure. They had boarded a raft to escape from the wreck of their ship. Where do humans come from? It's not so stupid to believe that we come from elsewhere, that we were in peril, and that our Earth is a raft cast adrift upon the storms of time. There is no tragedy more poignant than the true epic of the Raft of the Medusa. One hundred and fifty men lost in a raging sea. At the very outset some of them despaired and threw themselves into the water. From the very beginning there was a struggle for power. Who would give the orders? Who would obey? They fought, they tore each other apart with their sabres, ripped out each other's entrails. In the struggle they cut the cables holding together the beams that made up the raft. Food supplies and barrels of water were thrown overboard. While they were adrift the castaways dealt in arms. They stole food and wine. They threw their companions to the sharks. They took hostages. They cast the weakest into the sea. They were so hungry they ate their leather belts or hats. They drank their own urine. They ate the flesh of the dead.

By the tenth day of the shipwreck, the waves had subsided; all at once the black clouds vanished and the survivors saw a white butterfly overhead. By now there were fifteen of them. They pushed and shoved as they tried to catch the butterfly. Was the butterfly's freedom intolerable to these prisoners of a furious sea, scorched by hunger and by the salt of that sea? Were they so famished on their wreck that they fought over a crumb of nourishment flying between white wings? The butterfly continued its flight above the sea. If the story has a moral it is this: Life is like a butterfly above a raft laden with shipwreck victims.

ROCH CARRIER

And so I'm disembarking from our raft. Farewell. I am throwing myself into the sea. People will say that I've become a little crazy. They won't understand. Do I myself understand?

If a young man takes his own life he is seen as an implacable judge accusing society of being so rotten, perverted, decadent, insensitive, narrow-minded and boring that he can no longer live. When a man who has travelled all the paths in this jungle decides to leave it, it is suggested that his brain has shriveled, his judgment weakened, that he is suffering from tremendous fatigue, despondency, from an overall softening—all of which are understandable, given his age.

My dears, you should know that your raft too is threatened from beyond. An asteroid hurled into space long ago is heading for Earth. It will reach its objective with the same dumb intelligence as the most sophisticated missiles. In the past such an asteroid wounded our planet. One of those rockets that come to Earth every few million years caused the disappearance of the dinosaurs and of many other creatures that we aren't yet aware of. That asteroid is approaching at a speed of twenty-five kilometres per second. It is six kilometres in diameter. Its impact will be a billion times greater than that of the bomb that fell on Hiroshima.

Recently, a crowd of one hundred thousand from all over the world came to Mexico to observe a total eclipse of the Sun, the last one in the twentieth century. I was in Mexico on other business. With the economic developments that are on their way, Mexico will need pre-stressed concrete. "Forget about Montezuma and his pyramids, jump with both feet into the modern era and see that the future belongs to concrete!" That was the message I was supposed to deliver to the Mexicans. Over the years my stupidity has been worn down. I have less and less courage for proffering the kind of rubbish that was responsible for our company's growth. The workers who placed one stone on top of another to construct the soothsayer's pyramid at Uxmal knew more than the engineers who work with my famous concrete, which cracks like plaster and peels as if it had leprosy.

When I emerged from my meeting they announced that the eclipse had taken place. I saw photos of it in the newspaper the next day. I've always thought that work was the truest happiness, as much as love. That morning I was frustrated. I had missed the eclipse. There wouldn't be another until long after I was gone. While I was projecting onto a screen flow charts, statistics, and summaries of cost estimates for a pre-stressed concrete project, three stars in our galaxy were in precise alignment: Moon, Earth, Sun. The force that governed that incredible cosmological lottery is ineluctable. Who or what would be able to disobey it? Because the clock operates so precisely, somewhere there must be a watchmaker. I was thinking like Voltaire.

Watchmaker, my hour has come. I will have lived my whole life without knowing whether You really exist. Will I know after my Total Eclipse? (That's a little joke.)

You're telling yourselves, my dears: "At a time like this, with his life hanging by a thread, how can he try to be funny?" I would say this in reply: On this day when I am distributing my possessions, am I not entitled to have a little fun? Am I not entitled to talk about myself when I'm about to return to dust? Let the notary read my will. Be patient. Try not to fall asleep. Your eyes are heavy. Ah, what a pleasure it is for me to become unstuck from my pre-stressed concrete and to soar, to pirouette in my words.

I missed the total eclipse. I shall also miss the catastrophe that will be inflicted by the asteroid catapulted from the depths of space when it reaches Earth. I wish I could be there to observe the disaster! Is there anyone who possesses an imagination powerful enough to paint in all its colours his vision of an explosion that will extinguish life on Earth? Perhaps some poor lost wretch with his goat and ragged clothes and with seeds from the fields clinging to his rags, a hunk of cheese in his bag, will have taken refuge in a grotto in some backward country. Such persons will be spared. With their lice, their fleas, their germs, it is they who will be responsible for restoring life to the planet. Talk about the theory of relativity won't begin the next day. Life will start up again slowly, slowly, as it began. I won't be there. I would be glad if the asteroid that will bring death to everything that lives were powerful enough to bestow life on everything that is dead. I would like to live again... That won't happen. The closest thing I'll see will be my Pitiful Little Explosion against the viaduct.

Some years ago I was in Arizona. Or was it New Mexico? After a day of negotiations, I found myself in a barn where hefty cowboys were drinking beer by the gallon and listening to a scrawny mustachioed cowboy. He was wearing a big hat too, but he was drinking tea. He was reciting a poem about an electrical storm on a ranch. Don't smile, you with your refined educations. That poetry was more impressive than the French constipation of those poets you were forced to read and never liked. At the end of his poem the little cowboy said:

"Lightning is what God sends down every now and then to remind man of his place in the Universe."

Victor Hugo would undoubtedly have given a few francs for that idea. The modest lightning I'm going to spark won't be set off by God, but it will certainly put me in my place in the Universe.

The asteroid that follows its trajectory towards the Earth will put our planet in its place as well. What fireworks! It should really come on the night of the national celebration for our flag-wavers, full of patriotic winds and bigotry.

Humans, unite and declare war on that asteroid heading for you. From an engineer's point of view it is feasible to push an asteroid in another direction, to smash it into fragments and send them somewhere else. Countries of the Earth, unite, and bombard what is threatening you!

In the event that I emerged unscathed from the Great Massacre at the viaduct, I would leave the pre-stressed concrete I'm bogged down in and launch myself as an engineer of space: building exploration systems, inventing energy recovery networks, observing and analyzing conditions on Earth, erecting space stations, planning laboratories and factories for exploiting the resources of space, establishing recycling techniques for the disposal of terrestrial pollution in space... Ah, to be a space pioneer and set out with my tools and my techniques, like our ancestors, the pioneers of Canada.

When I was writing poetry, was it not because deep down I was in search of space—the space from which I come, the space to which I shall return? Instead of striving to grow wings, I chose pre-stressed concrete, that poor imitation of the good Lord's rocks. That material whose praises I've sung, that I've sold in such quantities, is as far from the rock's hardness as the wallpaper that imitated the Judean hills behind the Christmas crêche in my neighbourhood church. As for flying, my journeys have been unsatisfactory: an airplane is simply a big bus without wheels where they serve you overcooked chicken. It's possible that crashing into a viaduct is also a way of finally taking flight. I think I'd better change my plans. Instead of wrecking my

Jaguar, I'll borrow Melissa's Renault 5. It can still go fairly fast and I'll spare my Jaguar. I must check the insurance on the Renault.

My dears, soon I shall talk about the property that I'll leave behind after my passing. Just now, though, I'm trying to think a little. During my life I haven't often listened to myself think. I thought that living was something entirely different from thinking. Moving, bustling around, producing: that was the sum of my life.

Excuse me, I just received a phone call and now I must put this will in my safe. I have to go on a trip. Robert, my associate, wants me to go to Turkey. Our company is planning to build a dam on one of their great rivers, the Tigris or the Euphrates—Robert's not sure which. Iran, the neighbouring country, is protesting. Iran is afraid the dam will cut off its water supply. Iran is threatening to use fundamentalist terrorism and its armed forces against Turkey. With the very sketchy information he possesses, Robert wants our International Engineering Society, the IES, to propose a solution that would give electrical power to Turkey and water to Iran. This division of our planet into tribes makes no sense… I told Robert it was impossible for me to make the trip because of another project that's demanding all my time and energy. He wanted to know what it was. I didn't dare to tell him about my Great Resignation. I sat up and curried his favour like a ridiculous clipped poodle standing on its hind legs:

"You know, Robert, our highway viaducts are subject to considerable shocks. The standards that regulate the composition of concrete and the steel frameworks are based on data that reflect the conditions of twenty years ago. They're inadequate now, outdated."

Robert replied that he wished he'd thought of that himself.

"It's essential that we re-evaluate the work of the past if we want to remain the leaders in our sector," he told me. "We must continue to do the job that's too often neglected—to check where we're coming from so we can go farther and do the job better."

Robert could not postpone a trip to Japan, where the IES is involved in a plan to build a city on the sea.

"Their island is too cramped for their ambitions," Robert joked. "The Japanese aren't satisfied with an indoor bathtub any more. Now they want the sea in their basement! Victor, do me a favour, let me go to Japan while you go to

Istanbul. Let one of the young wolves carry on your study of viaduct resistance. He'll be glad to demolish the work of the previous generation."

I replied:

"In this life there are certain things a man must do himself."

Robert insisted:

"If you get a good idea in Turkey, Victor, you may be able to prevent a war."

Because of Robert's joke I decided to postpone my Final Move. I told him:

"Of course, Robert, I'll go and talk to the Turks, then I'll drop in on Tehran to convince the ayatollahs."

"Remember, Victor: We may quibble over the details but on the basic questions we always agree."

"Robert, I feel a tickling in my heart at the thought of building a dam in the valley where the first woman and the first man appeared."

Robert replied:

"I've always thought that the reason you're a good engineer is because you're a failed poet. Your pre-stressed concrete is embellished by the poems you haven't written... I'll see you after your trip... I've noticed, Victor...everybody else has stopped smoking, but you've started."

the end

I've come back, my dears. Sound in mind and body, I can continue writing this last will and testament to which you will allow me—I'm allowing myself—to add some personal remarks. When I was alive I talked to you more about my concrete than about myself. Now I want to tell you that there was more to me than pre-stressed concrete, that I also had flesh and a soul. During my lifetime I experienced a variety of feelings and I even had some ideas.

In Ankara I met the Minister of Energy Development and the Minister of External Policy. I also met Goulrisz—I assume that's more or less the way her name is spelled. She was responsible for some section or other in one of those ministries—and also for giving me a wonderful night. Like me, she was in a foreign country, because she was with me. Together we spoke a language that was neither hers nor mine. We were two lost souls, slightly pitiful, who had come from far away to be together for just a few moments. We'll never see each other again. We didn't want to miss that unique meeting. Love with Goulrisz was fragrant with yogurt, with fried food, brown tobacco and Chanel No. 5. At one point I felt that she was my only friend on Earth. I couldn't hide my secret from her. I told her about the Great Execution. Just then she was leafing through a magazine she'd taken from my briefcase: one of those magazines with a lot of pictures and not much text. You look at them when you're bored.

"You can't live any longer... Why?" she asked.

"Because with every season the fashions change. I'm tired of letting out my trousers or taking them in."

Her magazine was open to a page on which a young stud was exhibiting on long, catlike legs the beauty of a pair of trousers, tight around the ankles. When you're rather short and rather bald and rather pot-bellied, you hate men like him.

"Death is a decision only Allah can make. What you want to do is very wrong. Do you know what Mohammed says about the man who takes his own life?"

I was perfectly happy.

"I don't give a damn what all the prophets on Earth think. If God exists, He doesn't need all those prophets to speak in His name. Prophets are so long-winded. If they really believed that their God exists, they'd be silent. In their minds if they don't talk, God ceases to exist. Your Allah and my God have no need of prophets. And if my God or your Allah existed, They would be perfect. If They were perfect, They wouldn't have created imperfect beings like us, with our poor intelligence, our pitiful moral qualities, our diseases, our injustices, our selfishness, our fears and our foolishness."

"Allah is perfect and Mohammed is His prophet, chosen by Allah in His perfection."

"Do you think, Goulrisz, that a perfect God would be interested in us?"

"Allah has drawn up a plan for the Universe He created. He has a plan for each of our lives. Each of us is the carpenter responsible for carrying out that plan."

"So you believe, Goulrisz, that God has inscribed in his plan the day, the time, the place and the manner in which I am to depart this life?"

"Yes."

"And our meeting here in Ankara is part of Allah's plan?"

"Of course," Goulrisz assured me.

I've often thought about it since then. When an engineer faces the functioning Universe, he is forced to believe in a God who is an engineer. But God, the greatest engineer of all time, was a poet as well.

ROCH CARRIER

47

If God was perfect He didn't need to create the world. Why then did He create it? To correct His imperfection? Is not the Universe itself God? I shall leave for the Grand Vacation without having found the answer to those questions. Was the creation of the Universe His way of questioning Himself about His power, His vision, His focus, His sense of planning?

As for us humans, we arrive on Earth as total strangers. Like immigrants from another world we must learn the local language and habits. Then we become schoolchildren and learn what is contained in the memory of the world. Very soon we discover that teachers know nothing. And so, as strangers, we cross the bridge of our life, not knowing whence we come and or where we're heading. Most of us leave no trace. The strangers who will come later will never know that we were there before them. But it doesn't matter! If dinosaurs still existed, we'd lock them up in zoos, like the poor gorilla who kept throwing himself against the glass wall of his cage all day long, thinking he was leaping into space, or like the poor rhinoceros who tries to pierce the wall with his horn.

Nor does it matter that Earth exists: it is only one of the billions of things that float through space. It is inhabited by strangers who don't know where they've come from, who don't know where they're going, who don't understand where they are, and who pass through without leaving traces. I'll have left a few monuments myself, but that's of no importance. The concrete will erode like everything that exists on this planet. That's of no importance because such is life, as they say.

And so the execution of my plan for the Great Orbiting has been put off until next Wednesday. If it hadn't been for that journey to the land of Goulrisz I wouldn't be here now, writing this will. My dears, and you—lawyers, notaries, bureaucrats and associates—you'll have already started squabbling. Some of you will even have wondered: "Why has Victor done this to us? It's not his style. He was a successful man, a *bon vivant*." Yes, I love life! When you love life, or a woman, or a company, you mustn't linger. Why did I do THAT? Because I love life. I prefer to withdraw from life before it withdraws from me. "Why has Victor done this to us...?" I won't put too much emphasis on the answer. Does it really interest you? As strangers on the planet we are also to some degree strangers to one another. "Why has Victor...?" You'd like a simple answer.

Complicated people are always annoying. For you, then, here's a simple response. I, Victor Joyeux, engineer in pre-stressed concrete, being of sound mind and body, I have written THE END on the final chapter of my life for the following reason: I cannot do otherwise. I'm departing without knowing why, just as I came.

My dears, please don't say: "Poor Victor must have been depressed." Please, don't say: "Poor Victor has money problems, as well as his problems with women." And I don't have cancer or any other painful disease.

On the plane coming home from Turkey I found a catalogue. The cover was quite attractive. A golden young woman seemed to be waiting for me to call her and suggest a tennis match. The catalogue offered a list of tapes, "to help you live a better life."

Instead of writing up the report of my trip, I started glancing at the pages of the catalogue and reading the descriptions of the tapes.

> Videocassette No. 1: *Straight talk.*
> This tape teaches you how to talk when you are feeling anger, fear and desire.

That tape could be useful to me. I'm not confused about my decision, I'm just not sure how to talk about it. I cannot, my dears, tell you of my Great Future without beating around the bush. Is that too simple?... Endings are always so complicated. Birth and marriage are so much simpler than dying and divorce.

Videocassette No. 2: *Table manners.*

That one is useless. Eating is a pleasure. People eat in the same way they make love. Robert, my associate, is convinced that a man must be faithful to one restaurant, in the same way that he's faithful to one woman. In every city he visits, Robert always goes to the same restaurant. He never tries a different one. He never tries to find someone to help him sleep. My appetite was greater than my friend Robert's. It's too late to learn different manners. That chapter is closed.

Videocassette No. 3: *Your newborn.*

That chapter of my life is over too. Dear children, somewhere in the world you may have unknown half-brothers or half-sisters. To receive life is a privilege. To bestow life is an even greater one. Dear children, have children of your own. It's not true that Earth is over-populated: it is merely the victim of poor sharing, of dishonest management, of disgraceful planning, of selfish policies, and of religions that justify all those mistakes. Even if Earth is too small and the sea exhausted, the Universe has no limits. If I were sure that Melissa loves me, I would give her a child who would be company for her after I've gone. Dear children, I love you more than I've ever loved any woman, any dish, any fruit, any country. There are six of you, or seven, or perhaps more, and I wish I'd had ten, twelve, a thousand children. They are the most splendid creatures on Earth. With every child life begins anew. It's through you that I've received what life has given me. Thank you. You accuse me of having been an absent father. I assure you that always, ALWAYS, you were with me. Even though I am leaving, I shall find a way to remain with you.

Videocassette No. 4: *Focusing on marriage.* Marriage is the foundation on which the family is built.

If we were realistic, we'd try to find some other foundation for the family than marriage. Parents may divorce but the children do not. I have a certain esteem for marriage: I have married three times.

the end

Videocassette No. 5: *What women want their husbands to know about women.*

The main chapters deal with depression, low self-esteem, fatigue, tension, age and differing sexual needs which the majority of husbands usually don't understand. Too late! Too late! Too late! Even if I'd had this cassette earlier, it would have been too late. I've never understood, so I've been told in court, the depression, fatigue, tension, sexual needs and other problems of my spouses. They have never understood my fatigue, my tensions, my poor opinion of myself, my preoccupations or my sexual needs. Is not that beautiful, that profound mutual incomprehension the basis of marriage?

Videocassette No. 6: *Getting back together.* How to begin again a new and lasting amorous relation with your spouse.

NO. What has been lived has been lived. Time does not move backwards. The planet does not move backwards. What has been no longer is. Love is like a concrete bridge: when it's demolished it no longer exists.

Videocassette No. 7: *Falling in love again.*

53

I've been in love more times than I could learn from any course. To live is to love. I've even been in love with concrete.

> Videocassette No. 8: *Gaining the verbal advantage* (fourteen tapes and a guide). Do you feel that you talk in clichés when the crucial moment for talking arrives?

The problem on this planet is that too many people talk. The only useful tapes are the blank ones.

> Videocassette No. 9: *Control your weight through neuropsychology.*

What difference can my weight make at this point in my life? If I were twenty kilos lighter, under ideal conditions my car would come in contact with the viaduct a fraction of a second sooner. I'm eager for that embrace, but not enough to lose twenty kilos. I can achieve the same acceleration by stepping a little harder on the accelerator. The western world is obsessed with its waist size. For many people that is the horizon, and they can't see anything beyond it. They're obsessed by their diet as others are by famine. America eats like a pig and wishes it were as svelte as a gazelle.

the end

A fine civilization: *I eat, therefore I am.* Our continent has an upset stomach. For the future, our civilization is preparing a big fart. A long belch. Half of all humans are so hungry there are tears in their eyes. Here I am, as hypocritical as anyone else, giving you a lesson in morality. I've eaten more than my fair share of this planet's nutritional resources. I've fed my little belly, tenderly. I like to eat the way I like to love. My little belly has never been a handicap. Often enough it's been considered rather charming. Certain ladies have confessed that they can't love a man without a belly. Do you want to know if a man loves life? Look at the height of his belt. And so I don't want that tape about controlling your weight. That's another thing that should be announced to the world: Your greed is going to turn this continent into a desert. And your descendants won't have any trouble with obesity!

Videocassette No. 10: *Say goodbye to your backache.*

I've spent too much of my life sitting on my rear end: at my drafting table, at the board table, across a desk from a cabinet minister, in cars or planes. I have severe pains in my back. Didn't you know that, my dears? Haven't I bored you with my lumbar suffering? I confess as well that I've often wept in my hotel room. Wept like a lost child. And I was lost. I was weeping and no one could console me. Not even a lady of the evening. Have I never bored you with my pain? My backache will be cured next Wednesday.

Videocassette No. 11: *Say goodbye to high blood pressure.*

My doctor told me: "Your blood pressure is so high you're liable to explode!" Next Wednesday I'll show him he was right.

Videocassette No. 12: *Stay young through neuropsychology!*

My Great Action next Wednesday won't rejuvenate me. It will fix my age forever. Stay young? Why? What are the marvelous privileges of youth? Only the young can think that youth has advantages. Youth is foolish, ignorant, awkward, pretentious, narrow-minded, compliant, unreasonable, indecisive. Who would want to be young again? After a lifetime who would want to go back to being foolish, ignorant, awkward, pretentious, unreasonable, unstable, compliant, indecisive?

the end

P.S. Until what age are we young?

Videocassette No. 13: *How to stop smoking for life.*

Life is ironic sometimes. Here I am busily learning how to hold a lit cigarette to my lips. Cigarettes make me cough.

Videocassette No. 14: *Being comfortable with your arthritis.*

Some biographers claim that pianists who suffer from severe arthritis can feel their fingers loosen up when they touch the ivory keys. Under the same heading of miracle, in a bar I once met an old actor whom I'd just seen dancing in a country wedding scene. He had trouble walking. He explained that while shooting a film he'd broken both legs. He stayed drunk, he told me, to ease the pain. He could only walk supported by two canes. And yet in his role he showed himself to be a vigorous dancer. "On stage," he told me, "I don't feel anything." There are times when I have trouble closing my fingers around the handle of my briefcase. The pain is as unreasonable as a toothache.

Am I going to become all twisted like the old olive trees on the hills of Israel? There have been times when I was favoured with the miracle of the pianist and the actor. For me, though, the ivory is that of a woman's body and the stage is a big bed where I no longer know that I'm old.

> Videocassette No. 15: *You have the right to be rich.* Join the thousands of former pupils of Napoleon Smith. Learn how you can obtain in abundance everything you desire by applying nine easy principles.

It's more pleasant to be rich than poor, but the more objects you pile up in your cart the harder it is for the horse to pull it. Naturally I think that way because, according to some people, I am rich. Those people don't know that the rich man is always poor to someone else. My dear heirs, my fierce and loving spouses, all my sweethearts and you, my dear children, who are the gifts that life has given me—you, my dear son, in your mystical and financial community, you who refuse to see me because in your opinion I am a depraved father—know that there is more happiness in desire than in its satisfaction. Those who are truly rich are not those who possess all they desire, but those who desire all that they don't possess. (That's a rather well-turned phrase for an engineer.) My dears, you will be disappointed, you'll feel poor after I've given you everything I have.

I've never been poor enough to enjoy the ecstasy of desire, nor rich enough to enjoy the ecstasy of possession. I've been neither very happy nor very unhappy, neither very rich nor very poor.

If I am somewhat rich I became that way by chance. Wealth is a form of good health. And like health, wealth can be lost. Because it was given to me I've enjoyed it without tiring myself too much. Only once was I ashamed of it. Robert, my associate, and I had decided to launch ourselves on the adventure of collecting prestigious cars. It's more pleasant to drive a luxury car than a bicycle. Besides, when you've assembled several of them, you've become an investor. If you've made judicious acquisitions, the value of your collection can only grow. Depreciation can be written off. Etc. Ask your accountant, if you're really interested... And so, Robert and I formed a company. We rented a garage, we hired a mechanic, and we bought enough cars to fill our garage and keep our mechanic busy enough to need an assistant. Cars, like wines, have vintage years. We consulted advisers. We bought one car, two, five, ten. And soon we had nineteen.

Driving a rare car with a glorious pedigree gives you the same kind of vertigo as walking with a girl on your arm so beautiful that all eyes turn to look at her. You, my son who prefers boys, you'll never understand what I am saying. You won't experience the joy of being surrounded by light like God the Father because of a woman's beauty.

In the beginning we had as much fun as children with our new toys. It was wonderful to see gazes turn towards us. Even the most uncouth individuals are sensitive to the aesthetic appeal of a beautiful car. People respect them too: at times I've seen pitifully ordinary cars move out of the way so that I could park mine. Don't we spontaneously give up our place for a queen? And there have been times when I've found my car vandalized: a slashed tire, initials scratched in the paint. We couldn't parade around freely in our rich man's buggies.

When he learned about our pedigreed metallic steeds, our adviser almost fainted. "Those carriages of yours are like gold; would you take your strongbox out on the street?" According to him we were barbarians, ignoramuses, iconoclasts!

the end

We followed his advice and wrapped up our cars like fancy chocolates. And we travelled to Texas, California, Boston and elsewhere, surrounded by millionaires wearing evening dress like us, or low-cut gowns like our companions.

We were all very excited by these cars that paraded by like fashion models to the sounds of orchestral music. We were rewarded with a triumph whenever two of our jewels drove by: a green Opel 4/12 PS 1924, and the fantastic Rak 2, 1928, with its twenty-four rockets whose firing we simulated.

It was a competition. The purpose of one of the main trials was to select the cleanest car. The judge ran his white-gloved hand over the body, onto the motor, the cylinders, and under the car. The winner was the owner whose car had left the glove immaculate.

Those cars, I thought, were built to move us from point A to point B in superb comfort. But now instead of driving them we polish and clean them, we ream them with Q-Tips and dental floss, and we celebrate the cleanliness of the car that doesn't leave a mark on the judge's white glove! Caressing an automobile, sprucing and dressing it up, struck me as obscene, as incredibly perverse. It made me sick to my stomach. I felt ashamed. So ashamed that I wished I were poor. Robert, my associate, was just as disgusted. That night we decided to sell our collection.

On our way out of the exhibition a beggar asked us for change. We had nothing in our pockets. If my companion had given the beggar one of her earrings, he'd have been able to buy a mobile home.

My dear heirs, if you're worried that I'm not leaving you enough, perhaps you should acquire Videocassette No. 15: *You have the right to be rich.*

Videocassette No. 16: *The power of memory.*

After I've crossed the Great Viaduct, I would like to be visited again by the memory of Christiana returning her little fish to the sea; I would also like another look at the curtain in a child's sickroom, floating like the sail of an invisible boat, where I was protected and liberated from school. Those two visions of the Earth where I have been would suffice. I don't want to cultivate my memory. What's the good of remembering? People who remember do not live. I want to live my new life on the Other Shore, if there is a life there. When I travel, I travel light. As I depart Earth, I bequeath it my memories. Let Earth bury them!

the end

62

If my memory has not been completely erased from the invisible energy I will become, and if I must remember, I would choose:

a) the sugary red taste of a wild strawberry;

b) a few lines from the *Testament* of the poet François Villon;

c) my delight, as a child, at scoring a goal against an adult home from the war. That was my finest hockey game.

d) the tender little breast like an island where I ran aground on a night of failure and loneliness in the city of Paris;

e) the sky with its stars where I lost myself one night in Australia, when our little plane had broken down.

As for my concrete, it merits oblivion as much as the lines of verse I wrote when I thought my ego was so great that it contained the Universe. A human being is a great mystery, but how small that mystery is within the Great Mystery. I would like to be able to forget that I was once a small mystery within a great one. I would like to forget that I can remember. I want nothing to do with "the power of memory." I am leaving and I want the Great Door to be hermetically sealed.

ROCH CARRIER

63

Videocassette No. 17: *Goals: How to attain them.*

"Zig Ziglowski, the father of motivation, has helped thousands to define and attain their goals. He will help you convince yourself of what you can really accomplish," according to the catalogue.

Don't worry about me, Zig: next Wednesday I'm going straight to the Great Objective.

Videocassette No. 18: *Your power is unlimited.*

"Ten years ago," states the catalogue, "Tom Rabbit was unemployed. Today he owns a company with sales of more than forty-nine million dollars. He wants to share his experience with you. In thirty-one days he guarantees to give you full control over your mental resources and to unleash your personal power."

No one has power. Only life has. I don't like those who talk about power. They're only looking for submissive people. Do I have the power to prevent a minute cell from proliferating and devouring me? Do I have the power to retain my thirst for life? Do I have the power to think that wine is good, or life? Enough is enough. Only life has power over life.

the end

Videocassette No. 19: *Manage your time.*

Time doesn't give a damn about our agendas. Next Wednesday will come when it's ready. Wednesday. Why did I choose Wednesday for my Great Leap without a parachute? Why not Thursday? I don't remember. When Turkey kept me from doing what I was supposed to do, I put it off until another Wednesday. Why?

Videocassette No. 20: *The essence of success.*

What is success? Some say that I've attained it. I haven't noticed. Did I have success during that cluttered time when I had too many women, too many electronic toys, too many paintings, too many houses, too many jobs to do and too many employees?

The catalogue offers dozens of other videocassettes. All kinds of champions offer to: *Improve your golf, your skiing, your jogging, your bowling, your racquetball, sailing, surfing* and so forth. All I need now is to improve my driving so I can win my last Great Race. I must also perfect the art of smoking a cigarette without dropping any premature sparks onto my perfumed jacket.

My dears, this will is becoming as long as Victor Hugo's *Les Misérables*. Let me give you some advice: Don't wait until the final moment as I did to talk about yourselves. My life is marked with great gaps as if there were long periods when I hadn't lived. Those were the moments when I didn't take the time to realize that I was living... As for what you're really interested in, my dears, as for what you find more fascinating than my autobiography and my advice, as for the inheritance I'm leaving you, all the details will be found in the sealed envelope to be opened after you've listened to the reading of my will.

My grandfather used to tell a story that I knew as well as an old song. Yet every time I heard it my jaw would drop as if it were the first time. It touched me deeply, at a sensitive point hidden in the very secret shadow where tenacious memories take root. I was hypnotized by that story. No doubt I still am today, because it comes back to me just now as I'm about to live the final chapter in my own story, one that will perhaps be recounted too and that, perhaps, will fascinate a child not yet born.

The story took place in the country, a number of years ago. Everything was simple in those days. Progress, you will tell me, has prolonged the life expectancy of those people. Yes... What pleasure will they take from living to one hundred and five plugged into a machine? Progress will let you live to a hundred, but society shows that after thirty-five you're part of Antiquity and you should be somewhere else. Then you'll have nothing to do but go through exercises that loosen up your rheumatism.

At the time of my story everything was simple. An old man in my grandfather's village was tired of living. That's how the story began. What did it mean? I've never asked. My father always started it that way too. Today for the first time those words intrigue me. Was the old man worn out or sick? Was he a poor lonely soul whom no one loved? Had he come to the end of his cycle, having accomplished in his poor life what his poor destiny had ordered for him? Had he lost his pleasure in living? After a number of years on Earth was he drawn to the other life? Did he want to topple into infinity? Had he had more than enough of this life without pleasure? Had he suddenly become afraid of suffering? Did the world suddenly seem to him like a place he must flee? After having long accepted the days that were offered to him, did he rebel and say: "That's enough"? Had his soul told his body, "Old comrade, enough; I want a divorce"? Had the season for his death arrived like the season of snow?

One night at supper after he had eaten the sweet biscuit that he dipped in his tea, the old man wiped his lips and moustache with his napkin and said to his daughter-in-law:

"Wash this and put it away in the linen chest. I won't be needing it any more."

Now the old man often made remarks that weren't understood. The old man and his descendants lived together, but in different eras. They spoke the same language, but the meaning of their words was not the same. No one paid any attention to the old man, who went on:

"I'm going over to the Rocky Creek Road. There's things I have to do."

This was before the age of automobiles. The old man hitched his old mare to his Sunday carriage. He often said:

"When I see a fine mare, I feel that I'm still a man."

Later on, his descendants remembered having heard him complain that evening:

"Right now, even a fine mare doesn't interest me any more."

On Rocky Creek Road the old man stopped at the bridge. He looked at the water. A thread of water during this dry summer flowed through the grey pebbles, slightly orange now in the light of the setting sun. Beneath the bridge no one would have noticed the little stream, it was so thin and the grass was so high. The old man got out of his cart, he took his mare by her bridle and turned her in the direction of the village whose steeple and cross he could see. Then he pulled an envelope from his pocket and slipped it under the seat-cushion. And he took the whip and lashed the animal.

When the family saw the horse come back without the grandfather, they got worried. A child found the letter under the leather cushion. It was brief. The words had been written with the thick carpenter's pencil the old man always kept in the pocket of his shirt, over his heart, with a bunch of folded sheets of paper on which he scribbled incomprehensible things. The letter read:

"I'm giving you back my mare. She's the only person that can still put up with me. Look after her like she was my widow. God bless you.

"Your father, grandfather, great-grandfather, father-in-law who has lost his appetite."

Luckily the old man had muttered that he was going to the Rocky Creek Road. Immediately his children and grandchildren jumped into the carriage, while neighbours piled into others. With lanterns, rifles, bandages and rosaries, the whole village drove or ran or galloped towards the creek. Night was already falling; the shadows across the grass were getting longer. It seemed as if the lanterns were producing more shadows than light. When the night was the same colour as the spruce trees huddled together all around them, they realized it would be impossible to find the old man. So they decided to stop. "Listen, and then you can see," said the searchers. The forest was awakening. Night was stirring. Amid the crackling and creaking, the brushing and rustling and cries and sighs, they tried to distinguish the sounds of a man's presence. The old man wasn't calling, he wasn't walking.

The next morning three little boys were fishing in the rocky creek. They'd never get any trout here, they decided, the water was too low. The fish would need feet to make any progress here! Moving on, they spied a man lying on his belly in the grass. He was asleep with his face in the water. They ran to the village to announce that they'd seen the grandfather sleeping with his face in the river.

All the villagers, who were usually squabbling over politics, agreed on two things. First of all, at the place where the old man had drowned the water was no higher than soup in a bowl. Second, if the old man had drowned in so little water it was because he had decided to die. He had planted his face in the puddle of water and waited for the end. And so he had found the Great Sleep. It was that simple.

I have often thought of that story. I've often told it. The old man who brings his life to an end in a small amount of water is fascinating, like those saints who are supremely naive. My dears, even given the circumstance that brings you together now, I've taken great pleasure in telling you this story that I've heard so many times.

When it was being told it seems to me that life became very small, and the stream very large. I listened to every one of my grandfather's words, and I couldn't wait till he'd got to the point where he said: "There was no more water than soup in a bowl." It seems to me that the story was opening a curtain on another life that was hidden from the children. And yet he never failed to say: "There was no more water in the creek than soup in a bowl."

The grandfather had lived on little and he'd died on little. How simple life was in those days! The old man hadn't wanted to disturb anyone or anything. He had barely flattened the grass around his face. While I, I need to blow up a car and a viaduct along with myself. (You always forget something. Every architect has drawn a room without a door. I'm going to check my calculations. Will the cans of gas in my car be sufficient?)

My father, your grandfather, wasn't a happy man either. When he came home from his office at the Ministry of Agriculture, he didn't always deign to talk to my mother. Every day seemed to be worse than the day before. The Government was going to great lengths to make the wrong decisions that always went against the reports he'd written. His colleagues were jealous, his boss was unfair, his minister was incompetent. ("How can you draw up an agricultural policy when you've never held a cow's teat in your hand?") The Government was corrupt, the country was drifting towards bankruptcy, the world was racing towards a world war and the planetary system could not continue to turn without a fatal collision occurring.

Why am I telling you this? I am speaking to you, my dears, as if I'd never spoken to you before. I am speaking to you as if you had never listened to me. After all those years of concrete it gives me such pleasure to talk to you about something soft, something that won't last: myself. And so I'm not offering any apology.

I've lost the thread of this last will and testament. That's happened a few times lately. All of a sudden I couldn't remember what I'd just said or what I was intending to add. Sometimes at meetings I didn't know what country I was in or which project I was presenting. My plans, my slides, my documents seemed to belong to some foreign company. Recently I decided to call all women by the same name. Except Melissa and her mother. No woman is like any other and I remember every one. It's their names that have vanished from my memory. I forget to leave when I ought to; I forget to come back. Don't you think I'm ripe for the Great Oblivion?

Before I got lost, I was telling you about my father, your grandfather. To hear him, work was a kind of hell. With every passing day his boss was more inept. The system was becoming paralyzed. Every day, errors in judgment were more enormous than the day before. Unfortunately he was the only one who noticed they were heading for the abyss. Like a faithful watchman, he cried out: "Danger ahead!" but the others only cared about their personal interests. Ah, one of these days he'd write to them! He'd write to his boss, to his colleagues, the newspapers, the police, the M.P., the Prime Minister; he would denounce the intolerable situation, he would publicize the reasons for the situation. Oh yes, one day they'd know what happens to a man who stays silent for too long. Yes, he would write to them, "*tomorrow* at the latest."

He was in his office by seven-fifteen every morning. For us children it was a terrible place, a place where we weren't allowed to go. We didn't want to reach the age when we too would be condemned to work.

My father found a little peace at home. His suffering, the account of his dreadful days and all the bad news from the outside world made us give him as wide a berth as possible. Then he'd be there with my mother who would hear him out and say nothing more than:

"Yes, yes, you poor man."

And always, she agreed with him:

"Yes, yes, my poor husband, you must write to them."

At Sunday lunch my mother served up a roast of beef with vegetables. My father tasted it half-heartedly.

"Wife, this is the best you've ever made. It's

very good, but nowadays, because of the way cattle are fed, with artificial chemical feed and hormones to speed up growth and increase productivity, meat doesn't taste like it used to. This beef has no taste at all. People don't protest. They keep quiet and think they have to gobble up meat that tastes of plastic and newsprint. No one does anything. Like a bunch of slaves, they put up with it. I'll write to them one of these days... Wife, this beef doesn't deserve to be eaten on Sunday. Next week fix us a good roast chicken. Is there anything tastier than a good country chicken that's been roasted in its own juice?"

The following Sunday my father was carving the chicken as unctuously as a priest saying Mass with a deacon and a subdeacon. My father nibbled a little chicken.

"Delicious."

He chewed. We children waited to see what would happen next. We knew that the verdict didn't stop there. He chewed some more, then observed:

"This chicken is certainly a good chicken... People nowadays don't like nature. They think the good Lord made a bad job of His creation. Modern man thinks he has to correct God's work. Modern man is trying to produce square tomatoes so they're easier to pack into boxes. Biologists are trying to make lamb taste like fish so they can export it to countries that prefer the taste of fish. They think the good Lord made a mistake when He created round tomatoes and lambs that taste like lamb. This chicken, wife, is a good chicken, but my father and my grandfather would have refused to eat it. They'd have said that the meat had no taste. Children, this chicken has no flavour. If we hadn't actually seen the chicken, would we have known this was the meat of a chicken? This meat tastes like newsprint, like cardboard. It tastes of vitamins and drugs and penicillin—it tastes of everything they cram into chickens to keep them from dying before they've been killed. Chickens are treated so badly nowadays, they often die before they've been killed. These poisoned chickens are poisoning the population. People fear the atomic bomb. If you ask me, this chicken is more dangerous! This little two-legged bomb with spurs doesn't make any sound. All that chemistry... Can we control its effects on human genes? And the Government washes its hands! The politicians watch the people poisoning themselves. The chicken contractors are getting rich. The newspapers promote their unnatural animals. No voices are raised against this public damage. When everyone is silent, someone has to speak out. Let those chicken-murderers be warned, I'm going to write to them! If the people weren't such morons they'd rise up and demand chicken that's made not of rubber but of chicken flesh. For now, let us eat what we can. Next Sunday, wife, fix us a nice tender roast of beef. There's nothing like roast beef."

And so we grew up, from one Sunday to the next. If my father was unhappy at work I think that deep down he was no happier at home. He wasn't made for happiness. If there's a Heaven and if my father is there today, I know that he's not happy there. He would want to be on Earth. And because of my father I haven't spent much time at the school of happiness.

As for my mother, she held her peace. When my father was in the house his devoted servant was elsewhere to some extent. When I stopped being a child and thinking that I was the entire Universe, I wondered how my mother had been able to stand that dictatorship of sadness. In my father's absence the house brightened up. And my mother would smile.

What would she dream about when my father complained about the woes of the world and she was elsewhere, delegating a part of herself, a submissive and unspeaking servant, to answer the needs of an embittered man? At those moments of great sorrow when the life of the other was being stopped, what were her dreams? In what fantasy did she take refuge? In what house did she imagine she was living? With what man?… With what children?… From her I learned that real life is elsewhere. When life is no longer good, another life is always possible.

Poor papa! Children, never use those words when you remember me. I don't want you to pity me as I pitied my father. Considering Earth to be the worst planet in the Universe, judging our city to be the worst place in the Universe, declaring that humans were the worst creatures on the planet, threatening always to denounce evil and injustice, my unhappy father drowned in his own bitterness.

Perhaps I shouldn't judge my poor father. With his little diploma in agronomy he was unable to understand why everything was so complicated. Perhaps he simply despaired of ever having the strength to continue to hold up with his shoulder a world that would go on turning the way it turned for him. Was that why he urged me to become a lawyer?

the end

The country was brimming over with injustices and problems. According to my father, lawyers could tackle the injustices and politicians the problems. If the same man was both lawyer and politician, he would be ideal. My father had decided that I would be that person. He convinced me, at that time when children obeyed their parents and parents knew more than their children. I became a lawyer. I pleaded a few cases, I did some committee work for a political party. I enjoyed neither the discussions nor the squabbling. I always had the impression that the ideas I was supposed to demolish were more interesting than those I was defending. I was not happy. Instead I was worried about confronting a new life, as I'd probably been when I left my mother's womb. After years of legal language, I found myself deeply missing poetry. Suddenly I understood that the reason I was a bad lawyer was because I was a poet. I decided to become what I was. I set out to starve to death.

At every visit my father would reproach me for my long hair, my pallor, my skinniness. If I stayed for a meal he never failed to point out that I still had a big appetite for "food that's lovingly served to you at table." And he would add: "Food is something you have to earn." He insisted on reading what I'd written. I was not allowed to run out of inspiration. I had to give him some poems. Then he would wipe his glasses on his cotton handkerchief and read what I'd written, as attentively as when he read the instructions pasted on his medicine bottles. When he'd finished he declared:

"I can't understand why you don't write the kind of poems they used to write in my day. Poems that rhymed. I was something of a poet too, in my time. It didn't stop me from becoming an agronomist. My friend Plouffe, the notary, still writes poems today, verses with the hemistich in the right place, but that's never kept him from having a faithful clientele, or from eating his three meals a day and washing them down with good wine, at least on Sunday. I don't see why poetry should stop you from seeing reality. Poetry ought to help you see it better. With your education, you should go into politics. Poetry changes nothing but poetry, but politics can change the world. If you took up politics you could make life a little better for us. In any case I'm going to write the Government. Even if your place is in politics not poetry, it's unfair for young people like you to starve to death because they like poetry. A people should nurture its poets.

the end

They're like the good Lord's little birds. The day we have good politicians nobody will starve to death, not even the poets. I'm going to write to them. My boy, there's just one road for you and that's politics."

And that was how my father used to talk. When I knew his speech by heart, I stopped seeing him. I wasn't as hungry as he thought. A poet always has a steaming plate set down for him somewhere. For a poet there is always something to drink. For a poet there is always a pretty girl who likes his verses. The more the poet laments his solitude, the more friends he has. The poorer the poet's bedroom, the more friends come there to sleep.

It was a time when boys and girls shared everything they had and everything they didn't have. Those who had nothing possessed the others' possessions. One person's bed belonged to everyone. There was a lot of music. The talk was about love and peace. I wasn't writing much. Why write? So much poetry was already vibrating in the Universe. The libraries were filled with poetry like gardens filled with dried flowers. The popular singers were as great as Rutebeuf, as Villon. You only had to smoke a little something and the poetry would come and fill you like a new soul. Why write? As for politics, it was unable to make either peace or love. Politics was a deadly fiction. If we stayed aloof from it, politics would soon be metamorphosed by our dreams. All we had to do was dream a lot.

One night, we had gathered in a forest north of the city to celebrate the summer solstice. We wanted to honour the Sun, that is to say life, poetry, dream: the Sun-source, Mother Sun, the Universal Sun. We built an enormous pyre and lit it during the night to symbolize the immortal Sun. We had dragged dried trunks from the forest and arranged them in an arch, touching one another at the tips. The fire roared. Sparks fluttered in the black sky. Later, we no longer knew where the sparks were. Or the stars. There was lots of music. We drank. Smoked. We were dancing. Girls had come from everywhere. They wore flowers in their hair. They were beautiful. They danced like flames. They were so beautiful they didn't need their clothes. Like us, they tossed them onto the fire. Like us, the girls were smoking. They were beautiful like the fire. Their bodies moved like flames. We danced. We were inhabited by the fire: it was our soul. It was the feast of the Sun. Exhausted, we rolled in the grass, soothed like animals. The flames were not

the end

extinguished. We made love in the night. We made love, not knowing with whom. We made love with the fire, with the Sun, with the light. We made love with the first woman on Earth. We made love like the day and the night when they met for the first time, at the beginning of the world. And we gave birth to all the stars that burst from us in the night. The women's bodies were mere shadows and the play of red light.

Many children were there as well. To a small degree we were all their parents. They were youth, innocence: the original light. They had been put together in tents off to the side. Were they sleeping? Not all of the beautiful sparks had become stars. Some had fallen back to the ground. Some settled onto the tents where the children had been sheltered.

When I woke the next day to the violent June midday sun, I went for a walk and I noticed... I wasn't fully awake yet but my eyes were open. I spied a pile of charred scraps. I had meant to continue on my way. These black scraps had legs, they had arms. They were bodies—children's bodies. I screamed. I must have screamed, in the daylight, screamed horribly. I must have screamed like a giant, though I'm an average man. They heard me at the house in the distance, in the vans and tents in the field. Everyone was asleep. They were still drunk, lost, exhausted from the party. I had barely cried out when they surrounded their charred children. With dishevelled hair, naked because they hadn't had time to find their clothing scattered in the night, they sobbed, they cursed over the remains of the little victims who had been sacrificed to the Sun.

That same afternoon, I got in my Volkswagen and fled north, heading for Abitibi. I wanted to leave this life behind me. I wanted the open air. Very late that night I parked my car beside a lake planted with dead trees and I slept inside the car, barricaded against the clouds of famished mosquitoes. The next day I drove through forests, I skirted lakes in a great desert populated by spruce trees, until I finally came to some towns. I left them as quickly as I could. In those small towns they imitate what they think the inhabitants of big towns do. I kept driving, still heading north. Look at a map and you'll find, at the very end of the road that ended there, the name of Paradise. I could drive no further than Paradise. Along a gravel road that was more like a path, I spotted a house that had been abandoned years before, a deserted farm. I settled in for the night. I stayed the next day. I disturbed only mice and insects. I spent the week there, then the rest of the summer. Finally, I prepared for winter: I cut wood. I'd already harvested the vegetables in my garden. I got ready to hunt. During that glorious winter I was a kind of Robinson Crusoe.

The owner when he died had bequeathed the farm to his children, all of whom had fled Abitibi. They didn't want even to utter the name of their former misery. Then the farm was sold to a schoolteacher who had dreamed of escaping the noisy confusion of town, but he died during the first week of his retirement. At the funeral, his widow, who had never been very interested in emigrating to Abitibi, met one of her husband's classmates from normal school who was also retired, but alive and widowed… Finally, the farm was put up for sale.

In Paradise I was happy. I spent all day savouring the pleasure of feeling life within me. I thought sometimes of the life I'd left behind; my heart would beat very hard when I recalled how close I had come to the abyss. Those poor burned children had saved me. I was going to build myself a stone fireplace; I would put in new windows and write poems. Instead of being a pathetic lawyer who pleads pathetic cases for pathetic clients before pathetic judges, I was the king of

Abitibi. My life had become a poem. What is a word, even a beautiful word, compared with a tree, a stag, a pond, a breeze? I had discovered poetry—but poetry is an island where one is alone.

One night a man stopped. Representing a mining company, he asked my permission to conduct a geological survey on my land. I refused. He seemed to be so well informed, he must have already carried out his soil studies without my knowledge. He asked for a right of way to a neighbouring property. I refused. My legal studies were useful that night. When he left I was rich. Let's say, very modestly rich.

What does one do when one is rich? Try to get richer. Money, like poverty, makes us stupid. With my new car, in my new suit, my new Italian shoes, in new restaurants, I started to build myself a network of relationships.

How could I have been so happy on that farm at the end of the world? The thought of that isolated place made me shiver. There too I had come very close to the abyss. My entire life could have been lived there in Paradise, in Abitibi where summer was no more than three weeks long, where it was hard to grow even potatoes. But it is also the land of gold…

the end

Finally, I became a car salesman. A car salesman! I launched my message:

> If you're buying a car don't make the mistake of coming to me first. No. Before you do anything, speak to our competitors. Compare their prices. Negotiate. Discuss. Get the lowest price you can. Write up the contract. Before you sign it, though, remember me. And bring me that contract. You'll get the same car from me—but I will also give you a cheque for two hundred and fifty dollars, and my price is five hundred dollars lower than the competition's lowest price.

With all the fuss on radio and TV, it was impossible not to know about my business. The message was effective. It was heard. There was a rush of customers. There weren't enough cars to sell. There weren't enough employees, there wasn't enough space. The competition copied our methods. Our accountant got worried. I wouldn't listen to him. I sent him back to his office. He wore a toupee, my gallant accountant. When he was worried about something he'd scratch his head nervously and his fingers would shift the wig. During these hectic times it often sat askew on his head. A business, I thought, shouldn't be run by an accountant. Accountants are like thermometers: only good for telling the temperature. One morning the accountant came into my office without knocking. He'd forgotten to put on his wig.

"Monsieur Joyeux, I'm here to tell you that you're bankrupt."

I gathered up the money in my safe. After telling my secretary "I'll be right back," I made my way to the airport. A plane was departing for Zurich. I was prepared to go anywhere.

I abandoned my wife and child. In the early days of my car business I'd been dazzled by a customer's low-cut dress. She had bought a luxury car. She was rich. Her daddy was even richer. I phoned her about coming in for a check-up: "Don't risk driving more than fifty kilometres." She came back. Before night, we were in bed. A few months later the newspaper announced the marriage of a wealthy industrialist's daughter to a young businessman. Caroline, you were already nestled in your mother's belly. I abandoned you when I fled my bankruptcy. I wouldn't see you until later. I didn't really love your mother. I was too foolish. Your mother didn't love me either;

she didn't even hate me. I abandoned you, Caroline, as I abandoned your mother. I forgot you for a number of years. Suddenly you came back into my life and I loved you as much as a person can love when he regrets that he has abandoned a child. I loved you as I should have loved your mother. I abandoned you on that day, Caroline, as I shall abandon you next Wednesday. My final word for you will be: Love, Caroline, love; there is no reason to be on Earth except to love.

As for you, Annabelle, who had arrived before Caroline, I loved your mother very much. And yet I also left the two of you. In those days of long flowered dresses, of flower garlands and long hair, during those summers when making love was more agreeable than making war, in those intoxicating times of grass and music, everyone applied themselves to loving everyone. However, you can only love if you are free, and loving means that you're no longer free. We were all of us tormented by our freedom and torn apart by our loves. We numbed the tension that was deep in our souls, and that fatigue, with the smoke and music that were the rites of our fraternal tribe. Loving everyone, we loved no one. One cannot always give oneself; one can only lend oneself. Your mother, Annabelle, was like no one else. It was not enough for me to lie beside her. I needed to stay there. I wanted time to stand still. It was painful for me to leave her. She was the only one who asked me to read her my poems. Sometimes she would say: "That's one to keep."

Your mother, Annabelle, told me more than once:

"I'd like you to ask me to marry you some day."

I replied:

"When I've become a poet."

Then you were born, Annabelle. Were you my daughter? Even your mother didn't know. What did it matter? You were as beautiful as a poem and I loved you more than poetry. A few months later we celebrated the summer solstice. I saw the little black corpses in their burned tent. That morning you were laughing, crying, you were moving all your plump little limbs.

All the life that had been lost passed into you. I loved your mother, Annabelle, and I loved you so much, I could have spent the rest of my life watching you live. No other baby had laid claim to life as much as you. And yet I ran away to Abitibi. I abandoned you, Annabelle. It was my own life I was fleeing.

I found you again some years later. Your

mother didn't want to bring us together. She was right. One does not pass again through the gates of the past.

My dear heirs, I'm not telling you about what really interests you... I can hear you sigh, dear spouses, dear children. You don't care about my hesitations, my contradictions. Already you care little about a man who has just emigrated to the Great Elsewhere.

The plane touched down in Zurich. I didn't want to be in Zurich, with a suitcase that contained a razor, socks, underwear and a few thousand dollars. Just in case the accountant was right, I had stockpiled that money in my safe. And I stood there in Zurich with my suitcase in front of the big panel showing the imminent departures in white letters on black squares that clicked as they turned. What was I to do? I looked for a shop that sold postcards. I wrote to my company: "Forget me."

That day, a quarter of a century after my arrival on Earth, I was running away from my birthplace. My old father would not forgive me for having failed in my business. He had not yet forgotten that I'd turned down a career in politics. I was in Zurich. It seemed almost German, with its severe façades and its disciplined streets.

91

I wanted to be somewhere else. An airport soon becomes your home and native land. A crossroads that protects you from the aggression of the unknown. It lets you be anxious in comfort. Where to go? To Paris, of course. Going by way of Brussels: the Place du Marché, *frites*, mussels. And Amsterdam: the canals, the good beer. And then Paris, with its outdoor cafés where Hugo, or Baudelaire, or Villon, or Balzac, or Brigitte Bardot never appeared. I visited too many museums where the paintings were lonely enough to yawn. After that, Rome, with the extravagant palaces erected by Christians for a Jewish child born in a stable. Rome, with her girls as devoted as nuns. I was crazy. As soon as I arrived in a city I thought about returning to the airport and flying away in the first airplane available. I burned up my dollars. The whole world was a wheel of fortune marked with the names of cities. I spun it at random; they went past my eyes in a flash. Never did I stay behind long enough to remember: only enough to know that I wanted to be somewhere else. I felt as if I'd been skinned alive. The dazzle of a city pained me. Moscow: I imagined the city in flames before Napoleon's army. I sauntered past the sinister buildings where power seemed so sad. In Leningrad I walked along the Neva.

Why didn't I jump in? Did the sight of the steeple on the cathedral of Peter and Paul hold me back? I'd have liked to talk to those sad-faced people, but already I was on my way again. I wanted to travel faster than the Earth, faster than time. I didn't know what to do with my life, I didn't know where to go. I fled. I saw Beijing. Never had I been so alone. Why didn't these servile people jump over the Great Wall? I thought: The day will come when all the inhabitants of the entire world will resemble one another. Hong Kong. In Seoul I saw other slaves. At that time it was deemed intolerable to be a slave of communism but perfectly acceptable to be capitalism's slave. I travelled through many other cities. I could live without suffering only in airplanes and airports. On the ground I wanted to get out as fast as I could! Sydney, Rio, Istanbul. The world was a glass jar; I was the goldfish fluttering about as if he could go somewhere. London. A poet whose name I've forgotten—we forget the names of great poets but remember the minor ones—wrote that he had turned around like a squirrel in the cage of the meridians. I was going in circles. Trapped like the fish in Christiana's bucket. In London, I wandered. I wanted to be somewhere else. Among the pigeons in Trafalgar Square, beside a lion, I decided to come home. I had been happy in my wild domain in Abitibi, so happy I dared not go back there. I knew that the happiness I'd felt there was unique. I would find another refuge: a house like a boat set adrift, with windows looking out on the sea.

Of all that, my memory has recorded almost nothing. And I've left no unforgettable memories to anyone. I was merely a passerby on Earth. I didn't want to leave any traces. I wanted nothing to leave any traces on me. I was a blank canvas. I refused the responsibility of becoming a man. People who run away take no memories. Dear children, I was like some of you: I hesitated, I doubted, I blamed, I refused, I denied, I lied. My own birth, apparently, had been difficult. I didn't want to leave my mother's womb. After living on Earth for a quarter of a century I was still incapable of being born as an adult. I took refuge in the wombs of airports and unknown cities. I won't belabour the point. Children aren't interested in their parents' helplessness.

I was alone. Caroline, I didn't know where you were. Had I divorced your mother? Had she divorced me? We forget these things. Annabelle, I hadn't married your mother because people didn't marry in those days, but I'm fairly sure she divorced me when I ran away to Abitibi without her. I was so afraid, Annabelle, that you'd been burned along with the other children in the tent during that night of homage to the Sun. When I held you in my arms I was so happy to feel you alive! Pain wrenched my guts as if I'd lost you.

Upon my return I took refuge, alone, on the Magdalen Islands. Between piles of salt-smoothed lobster traps, I strolled along bays, among dunes, beside red cliffs. In the shadow of the lighthouse I let the wind and time trickle over my face. In that place where the river is as vast as the sea, I was flotsam. I was a piece of my time that had washed up there, in the rain, where the seals frolicked. In that haven, I spent hours watching the fishing boats. They swayed back and forth like someone who is hesitating. I had been happy in my house in Abitibi. I wanted a house. In the Magdalen Islands people are stubborn. They don't emigrate. Houses aren't for sale. When I showed him several thousand dollars on his table, an old man agreed to move into his daughter's house next door. I liked his white house that stood on a hill at the top of a cliff worn away by the sea. Small islands across from it seemed like leftover pieces of the puzzle of creation.

I repainted the walls. I planted flowers. I

sowed my garden. At last I would be a poet. Because of all that I had experienced, I thought, poetry would be born in me. It seemed to me that it was already there, that it was stirring, that it was disrupting my body like a child being formed in the womb. I just had to wait. And I realized that what I was waiting for wasn't poetry. I was hoping that a man would appear, as had happened in Abitibi, to tell me that gold had been found in my soil.

In summer, the boats spilled out noisy groups of young people who came to the islands for a good time. They played the guitar. They sang late at night on the beach. They made love under the stars. One day I spied Robert. He was busy building a sand castle with a young girl. It seemed to be a very serious venture. Robert and I had lived on the same street in the city, where our houses stood across from each other. We were old friends. Robert and the girl moved in with me. I told him a few chapters of my life. He was jealous of my memories.

"What are you going to do with all that experience?"

"Turn it into poetry."

"Choose something solid. That's what I intend to do: I'm going to specialize in concrete.

Pre-stressed concrete."

I laughed at that. Don't ask why, but at that moment my life toppled over. Some years later I had become, like Robert, an engineer in pre-stressed concrete. As for poetry, I never gave it another thought. Writing this last will and testament, however, is stirring up some old perfumes.

Robert and I studied together. We drank beer together. Robert never drank more than one glass. We hunted women together, but he always let them go. He was saving himself for later, he said. There was only one woman in his life. I used to tease him. "I'm like a great artist, I play just one instrument." Later on, I met some great virtuosos. Every one had a collection of instruments!

Montreal, a rather meek and mild city, all at once decided to stand up along with its villages. Montreal decided to grow vertically. It set out to become a giant among the giants of America. The frog wanted to be as big as the ox. And the animal would be made of concrete! We were ready, Robert and I! If God had carved from lava and rock the eternal pagan cathedrals of the Rockies, Robert and I would put up the towers of Montreal! Not only would we stand erect along with our city, under the vault of Heaven, we would dig tunnels under the ground and beneath the river!

My dears, you won't understand. I myself do not understand. I was more in love with concrete than I'd been with words in my poetic days, when I was trying to give the world a soul. I loved concrete the way I used to love the dough from which I made little rolls in your great-grandmother's kitchen. Concrete was a form of magic clay, of malleable granite. Robert and I were sculptors whose works would be inhabited by the crowd.

Starting then, there was always someone, in some country, who needed us. We were the missionaries of pre-stressed concrete. We built dams, we erected towers, we laid bridges across rivers.

I know, my dears, you're thinking: "He keeps writing and writing—when will he stop?" Deep down you're wondering: "When is he going to die?" I think about those years. I was more often in an airplane than on the ground, more often in a meeting room than in a house, more often abroad than at home. My father used to talk about how, in his childhood, he had dreamed over the pictures in a book called *Around the World*. Robert and I flew from country to country like my father turning the pages of his book. After our passage the cities were no longer the same: their profile on the horizon had changed, their shores had been joined, their narrow streets transformed into highways, their ground vibrated when underground trains sped by, their rivers harnessed to light the new towers, and their slums replaced by concrete buildings.

Each time we returned from our travels, Robert and I would have more employees on our payroll, more advisers, more accountants and always more lawyers. We needed more and more space: we built a tower… I'll say no more about it. That tower doesn't concern you because the banks have appropriated it for themselves.

We were the prophets of concrete. We accomplished miracles. I swore that if the pharaohs had known concrete, the Pyramids would have been built of concrete. Money was amassed like the water held back by our dams. The way money attracts women... Melissa wouldn't let me go on. She would accuse me of stereotypical harassment, as she's said before. She would denounce my prejudices, accuse me of having medieval ideas about women. To crown her insults she would conclude: "You have the mind of an engineer!" So to avoid irritating Melissa, I'll say instead… No, I won't say… And so we were rolling in money like swimmers at high tide. Women were there, on the beach. I loved them all. If I have wounded one, here, before I enter the Great Solitude, I beg her forgiveness. Even when they offered themselves to me, I desired each and every one. I loved every one. I gave myself to each of them as we give ourselves when we meet the person whose love will brighten our entire lives. Often I didn't speak their language but I would listen as if they had shared an important secret with me. When I think about a city I often see again the face of a woman. What can we know about a city if we don't know its women? Men all resemble one another, but women are unique. You haven't entered a city unless you've loved one of its women. Cities, countries, planet—I loved you because of your women, who revealed to me your most delightful landscapes.

Everything happened very quickly. Technology. Computers. Software. New ways of drawing. The boss has to make himself visible at times. I liked to go down to the drafting rooms and circulate among the tables, like a teacher who encourages, criticizes and, if necessary, corrects. The young engineers often rebelled against my suggestions. Their lack of docility pleased me. I noticed that I could no longer understand what my employees were drawing. My own art had left me behind. I confided in Robert.

"Why do we hire the best engineers in the world?" he asked. "Because we want them to be better than us."

In a restaurant one day I was in a hurry; I was leaving for Hong Kong. A place was free at the table of a broad-shouldered young man who was nibbling at a salad. I sat down with him. I ordered a double whisky.

"What field are you in?" I asked.

"Engineering."

"So you're an engineer...That's interesting...What's your specialty?"

"Pre-stressed concrete."

"Ah... I have friends in pre-stressed concrete."

"You've buried them in concrete?"

Besides healthy habits, he had a sense of humour.

"And how's business?" I asked.

"Business runs the way you run it."

"And your own firm, is it well run?"

"It's run by incompetents. The company is run like a bus going downhill without a driver..."

"That's sad. In the northern mountains of

Mexico, on roads as wide as the back of a snake, I've seen buses going downhill and..."

"You have to ask yourself sometimes where you're heading..."

"You're right," I said, "absolutely right. Where do you work?"

"I'm fairly new. I've only been there two weeks. I'm with..."

And he told me the name of his company. It was ours. "A bus without a driver..." I let him know whom he was talking to. And I ordered him to get off the runaway bus in distress. The young employee was probably right. A few weeks afterwards our business collapsed. It was quite an earthquake! We had erected a dam in Indonesia: an inspection bureau declared it to be dangerous because cracks had been found at its base. The lawyers hadn't been able to curb the government's demands. Then there was that bridge in northern Iran with an unstable roadway. At that particular time, I had just been arrested by the police in Toronto. I was driving home from a restaurant. I'd drunk more than one good bottle. My guest at dinner was the vice-president for public relations of our Toronto office. Why did she tell the police that I'd used my power as her boss to force her to go out with me? It's possible that I behaved badly like a man who loves women—that I'd been selfish, awkward, tiresome, disappointing—but I swear, I've never forced a young woman to go out with me. Even if there were as many women in my life as there are days in the week, I swear that I always approached a woman as piously as when I was a child in church, when I lit a candle at the feet of Jesus Christ to ask for the salvation of the world. Two beings, fragments of life that had come from so far away in mystery, after a journey that lasts millennia, meet for a few moments and create an invisible spark that will never be extinguished. That deserves respect.

In the next day's paper, under my photo, I'd become "the Casanova of concrete." My arrest for impaired driving and sexual harassment was reported. That same day, the bank seized our chain of sportswear stores. Robert and I had diversified. We were still in concrete but we'd gone into clothing, perfume, real estate, travel and tiles as well. And we'd taken on some art galleries, to make work for a few wives. Our negotiations in Russia were foundering in a maze of bureaucracy. The collapse occurred suddenly. It was like winter: you're walking on the firm, solid, white earth. All at once, a patch of ice hidden by the snow. You slip and fall.

I didn't feel like starting again. My dears, don't think that I've succumbed to depression, to despondency, to despair. My life has been what it's been. I'm happy with the way it has been. It could have been otherwise but I didn't wish it to be otherwise. I've finished. Enough concrete! Enough negotiations! Enough travelling! Enough women! Enough raspberry jam on my toast at breakfast! Enough! I've seen enough of this world. It's time to exit through the Great Door.

The ashtray is full of butts. I've learned how to smoke again so I won't spoil my departure. I loathe the smell of tobacco ashes. I loathe my own smell too, but I'll go on smoking until my last second.

Are you crying now? I'm not, though I am leaving you. I am making my departure like someone who leaves the table after a good meal. I won't come back. I like the religious promise that the soul survives the Great Exit and continues travelling at the speed of light as it passes through walls and barriers. Unfortunately I don't believe in it.

You, William, for years now you've refused to see me. You'll be sorry you didn't speak to your father while you were both on the same planet. I know that you'll start talking to me again as soon as I am part of the Great Anonymity. You judge me harshly. I probably wasn't a good father. William, you're right. I'm probably guilty of all your accusations and of a few others that you'll make later on. You, my most pitiless judge, will be the only one who sheds tears when you learn of my departure. Like you, I was harsh with my father. And I cried when he left us.

Your father, who has caused you so much pain, was just a poor man who groped his way through life, not knowing what was good, what was bad, what was or was not important. I was nothing but a very lonely man. It's possible that work has been the only God I honoured. I may have been a bad father, William. I'm sorry. Know, though, that I was just a little guy trying to survive. I tried to find a meaning for all that. I didn't find one. William, my tormented son, perhaps you won't find one either. You will shed tears. And I'm shedding some tonight—it's so late—as I write you this.

Tristan, I love you too. I don't understand. I, who have loved women so much, have produced two sons who do not love them. What a waste! What a loss for women! You are the two most attractive men I know. I don't understand. You tell me that your orientation is explained by a conformation of your brain. Did you inherit it from me? Did I have delinquent cells? If that conformation of the brain is congenital, does it mean that all my life I've run after women without suspecting I was homosexual? I don't understand you, but I love you. However, I still maintain that I'm entitled to what you call my prejudices. In my next life, on the other side of the Great Viaduct, perhaps my soul will have the power to wander where it pleases. If I should see you, my dear sons, wearing lacy brassieres and panties, I reserve the right to burst into tremendous laughter from beyond the grave. And after that perhaps I'll wipe a tear from my invisible face. What a mistake: not to accept the pleasure of being men! I don't understand you, but I love you.

My dears, it is very late. It's finished... I've written too much. My eyes are closing. I don't want to go to sleep without drawing up the plan for my last day.

Before that, I assure you that I'm not leaving the Earth because I'm unhappy. Don't blame my collapse. I'm as stupidly happy as a man who has just stuffed his belly. Isn't that the most appropriate time to make the Great Leap? Why should you want me not to disappear till I've been tortured by physical or mental woes? I am leaving when I'm still happy. My bankruptcy? It's not mine but my company's. I could begin again. The more idiotic the world is, the more concrete it will need... Yes, I've lost a great deal... It's not in my nature, even if I've lost everything, to lose myself too. I still have Melissa, her mother, a few memories, a few possessions and other objects of which I will give you a list, my dears, if you'll just be patient a little longer. Don't think that I'm leaving to get revenge on that dear crook who, after he'd ruined us, built himself a castle in the hills of Provence.

Here's what I'm going to do on my last day. Perhaps I'll write a little more to you? Since I've been drawing these little curls of words, my departure is less urgent. I want to see Melissa. And after that I want to see her mother... I sense your disapproval, my dears. Your father, that bald old man who coos over an adolescent girl and later over her mother...You're disgusted with me. I don't give a damn! Give me back my youth, if you can, the way Melissa does! With her, I'm the same age as she is. Give me something as good to touch as her muscular athletic shoulder. Give me something as good to look at as her eyes that aren't yet tired of life. Give me something as good to feel as the warmth of her breasts against my chest. Invite me, as Melissa does, into the magical garden of youth. Give me, as Melissa's mother does, the serenity of one who knows that life has the raging force of the sea. Good night. I'm going to bed.

I slept well for an hour and a half. Then I woke up. I'm not sleepy any more. For me, the night is over. I would like to embark on my last day right now. It seems to be refusing to arrive. Am I to think that the day is refusing to come because I am leaving? Whether I'm here or not the Earth will turn, leaves will stir in the breeze, there will be traffic jams on the bridges, the morning paper will be published. Tonight I am already somewhere else. I am at the side of life. I am a spark cut off from the candle's flame; I am burning for a moment now before I am snuffed out. I am thinking of nothing. I am thinking only of a black and silent and dense night. I am thinking only of that Night where no one thinks. Final Night. Great Night. The one where I shall be tomorrow: the Great Night where no one awaits the day.

They say that during those waking moments before the end, you see your life unwinding like a film. Who can say? Who has come back from such circumstances to tell about it? On the black screen of this night no image is projected. I no longer know if I want to remember or if I want to forget.

In the shadows, lit by a candle, Melissa, in her narrow student's bed, unfastens her brassiere to offer me her breasts. My hand feels her young heart vibrate. Suddenly it is in as much turmoil as my own old heart... I am going to leave Melissa. Dear Melissa, don't cry! No, do, do cry! You'll forget me. You will love someone else. And you'll cry again because we only love what we lose.

When I'm gone you'll go to your mother's to cry. In her arms. You will rest your head on her shoulder, in the same place where I've often rested mine, you will take refuge on that bosom where so often I've found peace after returning from those adventures so tired that I was incapable of love. If your mother is in tears, Melissa, don't ask her any questions. Let her cry. Cry, both of you. On this last night I am thinking of you; you are with me here in this solitude of time that has stopped passing. Through the lawyer's mouth I swear that I love you, as if you were one. With Melissa I could be my own age and with you, her mother, I could be the age of Melissa.

ROCH CARRIER

109

I cannot sleep. I don't feel the slightest fatigue. I've spent so many nights at work: drawing, analyzing plans, preparing presentations of projects. I wish I could do nothing, but the weight of this night overwhelms me. I look out at the city, behind the blue gauze of night that soon will be drawn by the morning. It is three minutes before three a.m. I don't feel like dying. I don't feel like living. I'm not hungry. I feel no desire. Could I be happy?

Before I leave the planet, I want to write a few more words. My dears, because I was absent so often, I have spoken little to you. When I was with you I was still in the world I had left, or already in the world that awaited me the next day. Projects, plans, negotiations, strikes, defective machinery, stolen materials, poor quality, deadlines: in your lives, I was a preoccupied and distracted man. Tonight I am writing to you. I cannot speak to you because I'm already far away. Oh, this night weighs on my shoulders. It weighs because it does not end. And yet I know it to be light. It seems to barely brush against the Earth. After I've crossed the Great Frontier I shall be even lighter than the night. If my soul does not crash into the viaduct, it will continue to soar in the night and in the day. Have I undertaken, with all the words in this last will and testament, to write that poem I dreamed of writing so long ago?

Why sleep? Will I not, at three o'clock this Wednesday afternoon, take my Great Siesta?

I no longer desire anything. My life has been beautiful. God, if You exist, I thank You for it. I am satisfied. I'm no longer hungry. Do you really insist on knowing why I've taken my Final Bow? It all happened because of my little finger. For some time now I've had an acute pain there. Is it arthritis? Let's say that I wanted to escape that pain in my little finger. Or else it might be thought that I've succumbed to the pain of living.

A lot of butts have accumulated in the ashtray. I haven't got used to smoking. I don't like smoking.

I am alone now as I was in my mother's womb. In a certain fashion I will soon be born.

My eyes are full of sand as they used to be when I stood too close to the cement-mixers at job sites. My eyelids are heavy. My eyes are dry. Will I have that sensation when I tumble into the Great Dream? I am looking again out my window. The city is there, indifferent, as though nothing were happening. And yet in a few hours the newspapers will recount its nightmares. The city is indifferent as if nothing were going to happen to me. It is indifferent as it was when I was born. It is indifferent as it was indifferent on those days when I was not about to cease living. Why am I irritated by the city's indifference? Should the city be tense because I am tense, like a thread that is about to break? I have lived amid indifference. I have been indifferent. My friends, associates, partners were nothing but masks of indifference. Tonight I am in a sense gazing at my soul, which soon will dissolve into the Great Indifference. Why should the city not be indifferent to me? What importance do I have? You will say, my dears, that I was beset by acquaintances who took the place and time that you laid claim to. You'll be right. I have been loved more than anyone. I have loved more than anyone. There have been times when my soul was tired of love. The night is gliding softly into the day. Without me as with me, it will be what it must be. This morning I am alone on my drifting boat. How many will surround me to stop me from plunging headlong into the Great Fall?

My feelings are becoming confused. I should sleep. If my mother could see me she would say:

"You look terrible! As if you've lost your best friend! You have to put something in your stomach. Here, let me give you a piece of strawberry pie with cream. Now, now, you can't go to sleep on an empty stomach. It's just cream, strawberries, flour: all natural! And there's nothing like nature for restoring life..."

My poor old mother...she cures all your ills with dessert and cream! If she were to turn up this morning with her strawberry pie and her cream I might well be cured!

I'm coming to the end. My dears, you've all gathered at the notary's office to hear him read this will. I've taken the Great Leap without a parachute. Do you not understand? Do you think I understood? In the great storm filled with wind and night that is the world, life is given to you like a candle's flame. I've made the decision to extinguish it myself. The night was too big and my flame was too small. Had I become obsessed by the night? Did it attract me more than this wavering brightness? Some mosquitoes are drawn to fire and burn their wings when they come close to it. Mine I have burned in the night. I'm going to bed now. Good night, my dears.

I slept as if I had nothing else to do. The phone didn't ring. It was as if my number was already out of service. I thought I should go to the Ritz. It was late for breakfast but perhaps some friends would be late too. After that I'd come back to make my preparations: fill my gas cans; make sure I have at least one cigarette to light; put some matches in my pocket in case the car lighter doesn't work. I won't be able to fill all my cans in one place. I'd risk being noticed. I'll go to a number of gas stations. I'll bring just one can at a time. And I should borrow Melissa's Renault too. It would be a waste to destroy my Jaguar in this operation. I won't talk too long to Melissa. She's young but already a woman; and women are too good at reading faces and eyes. I don't want Melissa to know.

I had dreamed of a more interesting final day. It was coming along like a day that will be forgotten. A day that seems not to have happened.

A long time ago I read a story about an old Spanish noble who, before he took his life, wanted to do everything the doctor and his age had long forbidden: drink wine, go to a brothel, get on a horse and go hunting. What panache! Alas, for my own last day, I'm a theatre director with no talent, an author who can't find the words to express tragic beauty.

At the Ritz I spotted Robert, my associate. He was at a table by himself. Our collapse has changed his schedule too. Robert seemed surprised to see me.

"So you're not too busy either," he said.

"I'm as free as if it were my last day!" I replied.

"You know," he confessed, "I've done nothing since the events. I haven't taken a single phone call. I haven't read a letter. Especially not the ones marked URGENT. You may not believe me, Victor, but I've even considered suicide."

"Not you, Robert! You're energy personified!"

"After our collapse I had no challenge, and therefore no energy. I made plans for a painless disappearance. You know how I dislike suffering."

"In circumstances like this people tend to see everything in black. To exaggerate. To think they're being abandoned. They think they've failed at everything. But dammit, they're still alive! Is anything better than life?"

"It's easy for you, Victor; you're a born optimist."

"Yes, of course. To tell you the truth, Robert, I have to say that the thought of suicide has never crossed my mind."

"My dear Victor, I've put everything in place for my own disappearance."

"Robert, a man like you doesn't need suicide."

"Victor, as you know I haven't always approved of your lifestyle: all those women, your international harem..."

"Robert, as far as I'm concerned you didn't love women enough. If your life is filled with women, how can you even think of leaving it?"

"Victor, I know you've never stopped being a poet. You've always been a poet disguised as an engineer."

"Robert, what I love is concrete. After all these years, even after our collapse, I'm still passionate about concrete. I have an irrational love for that material. It's the material of the century! A material we've barely discovered: we only know the first notes of a symphony! Concrete is a beast we haven't tamed yet. Robert, the world needs concrete. The world needs us! Robert, our past was in concrete. Our future is in concrete too!"

I was pleading in favour of life. On this final day I wanted to be useful to my associate. I wanted to do him some good. I wanted to save his life.

"Come with me, then, Victor! At twelve-fifteen there's a talk about concrete at the engineering school. I'll take you. It will be like the good old days, remember, when I converted you to concrete?"

"I have an appointment this afternoon that I can't miss."

"An appointment you can't miss? I respect that. Good old Victor! What's her name...?"

"Robert, you know that love's more durable than concrete!"

Just then I'd have liked to confide my secret to Robert. We had lived a lifetime together. We knew everything about one another. We had built the company together. We'd brought up our families together. Our children used to say they had two fathers. Together we'd experienced success and failure. What, then, was keeping me from revealing to Robert that most essential project? We mustn't let our deaths trouble those who go on living.

"Victor, I sometimes reproached you for not influencing me a little more. You know there's been only one woman in my life—my wife. I've been faithful to her the way one is faithful to one's church. Perhaps I should have sinned a little..."

"You still had your passion for concrete! And I have to say, Robert, you found *the* woman. I'm still looking for her."

"Victor, in spite of all your fantasies you're serious. You never lose sight of what's important.

Let's go and hear that talk about concrete. Does your appointment matter as much as you say?"

Would you have refused to go along with my old associate? At the engineering school we listened to a denunciation of concrete. According to the speaker, contemporary man is an ignoramus who knows no more about concrete than did Cro Magnon man. At certain periods in antiquity, man knew how to produce concrete that resisted the violence of the ages. Those secrets weren't passed on to modern man. The knowledge of concrete has been lost in economic perversions where profits are prized more than art. In contemporary times, concrete is no more resistant than clay. Our bridges are afflicted with gangrene. Our building foundations are rotting like fruit. Their walls are cracked. There are fissures in our dams that grow wider day by day. Highway interchanges only hold together because they're used to traffic jams. Modern concrete is a failure, a bankruptcy. Our generation will have brought many builders together. Burning with ambition, we've built castles of sand. That's the modern tragedy: our concrete is nothing but wet sand. Concrete symbolizes the failure of modern man who has forgotten the art of building. Our modern concrete is stricken with a cancer that is eating away at our cities. Concrete is shit that stands erect because that's how the architect designed it. If our populations knew how dangerous it is to live in their gangrenous cities, they would emigrate to the country. Even there, they wouldn't be safe. On the steppes, in the tundra, even in the desert, dams are threatening to split open. On the outside, the concrete has leprosy. Inside, it's as soft as mud. And that's what is responsible for holding back gigantic masses of water. It's to them that we entrust the passage of trains, buses, trucks, cars. It's to them that we entrust the sheltering of millions of people.

"Citizens of our towns, prepare for avalanches of concrete. Human crowds, stay away from stadiums! Modern engineering has produced a concrete whose soul is disintegrating along with the body. A world to be rebuilt: that's the heritage we're leaving our children, some of whom will be victims of concrete! The survivors will be the phantoms of our ruined cities. That is where human technology has brought us. Already our structures are the ruins of an era that is not yet past. Concrete is the disease of our century. It's too late. We cannot mend our failures. Gentlemen, be prudent, if you see a viaduct don't drive over it or under it!"

"Feeling better, Robert?" I whispered.

"Victor, we're a success!"

We left the room more quickly than we realized. Our colleagues in the concrete industry were slumped in their chairs, heads drooping.

"I'll sue him," Robert threatened. "I don't intend to let that moronic rabble-rouser throw our whole life out with the trash."

"What life?"

The words had sprung to my lips without my consent. That wasn't what I'd meant to say. Our concrete wasn't that bad. Our accuser probably had bad breath and stomach cramps. My life hasn't been that bad.

"Victor, you're smoking," said Robert, surprised. "You've started again? Smoking is dying by inches—you know that."

"Don't worry about it. My lungs are as solid as concrete! Robert, I have to be going now."

"All right. See you soon!"

He held out his hand. We were about to go our separate ways as usual. But this wasn't usual. It was the last time. Robert had already turned away. Robert was my brother, my father! I would never see him again. He didn't know that he'd never see me again. What came over me? All my life, feelings have seemed so indecent that I hid them in my poems. All at once I rushed over to Robert, who was amazed to see me go up to him, my arms flung open.

"I want to embrace you!"

I took him in my arms, my cheek against his, then went on my way, my eyes filled with tears. He said nothing. What I needed was a stiff whisky on ice at the Ritz. After that I'd phone Melissa and her mother. Then it would be almost three o'clock. Farewell, my brother, my companion!

At the Ritz bar I ordered a double whisky.

"A Glenfarclas as usual, Monsieur Joyeux?"

"That's my favourite brand too," said the woman next to me.

I had noticed her red leather suit. I'd probably been drawn to this seat by the tight-fitting leather. Her back was inviting; so were the long legs, folded close together.

"This is my last whisky," I told her.

Once again I felt that tantalizing need to share my secret without revealing it, to say it without saying it, to pretend to tell it, to reveal it by concealing everything.

"If you're going to stop drinking," deduced the woman in red leather, "you must have a good reason…"

"When the time comes to stop, it's time."

"You're one of those men with an iron will... Waiter! Two more!" ordered the woman in red leather. "We're celebrating the last whisky of Mr...."

"Joyeux," I said.

She couldn't pronounce my name; she mangled the syllables.

"Joyeux means happy!"

"Cheers, Mr. Happy!"

"Happy—that's saying a lot. I'm committing suicide today."

The lady in leather burst out laughing.

"You, Mr. Happy! One look at you is enough to know that you're condemned to live. You're the liveliest suicide I've ever seen. Think it over: suicide is like marriage. It's for life."

My dears, you don't find that joke very funny. You wish the notary would stop talking. At the bar of the Ritz it seemed very funny indeed.

"What type of business are you in?" she asked.

"Concrete."

"Concrete?"

"I'm an engineer in pre-stressed concrete."

"That's solid."

"And you?"

"I'm in humour the way you're in concrete: I'm a humour therapist. My company has developed a hundred humour-related products. We have books, tapes, videocassettes."

"Tapes. Videocassettes...how interesting!"

It has often happened that I've been captivated by an absolutely banal conversation with an unknown woman.

"We offer humour workshops, panel discussions, lectures, correspondence courses. Haven't you heard of our series: *Using humour to fight shyness, boredom, pain, fear of death, marital tensions, depression, toothache, frigidity and aging?"*

"With humour?"

"Our company has sales figures in the millions. Our latest release is *Fighting the effects of divorce with humour*. It's the sequel to *Saving your marriage with humour*."

"Tapes... Do you have anything on suicide?"

"Not yet! Suicide is an absolute absence of humour. Have you ever seen the look on the face of a suicide victim? It's no laughing matter. Suicide victims think that Earth is a horrible place, that humans are horrible creatures. Which, just between us, is true. If he had a little humour the suicidal person would smile at life instead of grimacing, with a rope around his neck. Unfortunately, suicide and humour are incompatible. Nothing is interesting or important to him. He's indifferent to everything: even life... Are you all right, Mr. Happy?"

That red leather suit contained treasures. I invited the lady to eat with me. I don't know how or why, but suddenly we were in her room and we were laughing like children. She knew I had an appointment at three o'clock: she was delivering a speech at the same time. Oh, how the leather hugged her curves, as tightly as a cellophane candy-wrapper.

"Later!" she suggested, pushing away my hand that was advancing like Napoleon through the Italian hills and the Russian steppes.

"Later." Life is so short. And she didn't want to hurry. I've never been able to tolerate being told "Later." There's no such thing as later. Later never happens. All that exists is the furtive flash of now. That was why I told her:

"Later...at three o'clock this afternoon I'll be dead."

"Do you really want to commit suicide, Mr. Happy? Are you constipated, darling?"

She was gazing at me as if I were about to reveal a state secret. She pleaded:

the end

"Tell me…"

"NO, I am not constipated."

"You're not serious about suicide, Mr. Happy. A recent study shows that over ninety-one percent of suicides had been suffering from constipation. Instead of hurting yourself, Mr. Happy, why not come and hear me speak?"

Don't ask me why I went with her. My last day was going to be truly educational.

The room was filled with ladies holding humorous books and videotapes on their laps.

I feel that kind of sympathy for vulgarity most men experience when it's found in other people's wives. My new friend had led me to the front of the room, to the first row of seats. Before she spoke, she rested her hands on the lectern and leaned forward. At the sight of her bosom I, the only man in the group, felt as dizzy as I'd been before the Grand Canyon.

"Ladies, humour in your life is an umbrella in a shower. Nothing is totally sad. We never lose anything. After my divorce, I wept: I had lost the man of my life. My pillow was soaking wet. Then all at once I thought: If he's not there any more, neither are his socks. I won't have to pick them up any more. His pillow was dry. I laid my head on it and fell into a sleep as sound as if the judge had awarded me one hundred percent of the possessions of the former man in my former life."

The ladies applauded. People are so lonely, they'll listen to anything. Even when a woman says nothing interesting, she is still fascinating. And so I stayed in my chair. The audience was hanging on the lips of the lady in leather. Which were undeniably generous. In her eyes, a tumultuous life had undoubtedly flowed and polished them very smooth. Her hair was a feverish torrent of blond curls. She stood there, sturdy, at the mid-point of her life. She said what she thought. She seemed to be saying: "This is what I have; it is modest, but I'm offering it to you." And her body like a bowl of peaches... Ah, I think I know why I stayed. It would soon be three o'clock. Too bad, I'd be late.

"Ladies," said the speaker, "humour turned my divorce into a holiday...a paid holiday... paid for by my ex-husband. Do you know why marriages are less successful than divorces? Because marriage requires the husband and wife to live together."

I, who had decided not to wait for the end of my days, waited patiently for Her Red Leather Majesty to finish her speech from the throne.

"Humour works miracles. Listen. Just today

I witnessed a miracle... Today, I drank three whiskies. With the first, the man who offered it to me confessed that he was going to kill himself as soon as he'd finished his drink. I offered him a second one, with some humour on the side. At the third whisky, my potential suicide victim had recovered so much life that he began to undress me... Why, ladies, do we wear pretty underwear? So someone will take it off, isn't that right? (Applause! Laughter!) That man who was going to kill himself was undressing me! My ex-husband, who claimed to be alive, hadn't done that for a long time!"

There you have it. I'd become her suicide victim. Like an idiot, I sat there glued to my chair. The Great Lady in Black could wait.

Was I suddenly afraid to die? Yes, I was afraid. And all at once I remembered clearly something I'd read in the book of Buddha long ago, in a hotel in Asia! One day, a man was rowing his boat along a river with a powerful current. Someone called out from shore:

"Stop rowing in that choppy river so cheerfully, there are rapids, there are dangerous eddies. Further along crocodiles and demons lie in wait in caves. If you go on you will perish."

The man on the shore was Buddha.

ROCH CARRIER

No one had told me, "Victor, stay away from those perilous rapids." No one had noticed that I was rowing through water that was taking me towards the Great Caves. The lady in red wasn't Buddha but she had spotted me, she had spoken to me. Was that why I hadn't run away? My dears, sometimes a man is very lonely.

A TV crew came into the meeting room. No sooner were the lights turned on than the lady in red leather told the camera:

"Thanks to humour, my divorce has been happier than my marriage."

She was strong, stronger than I had realized. She made her way towards me, holding out her hand with its luxuriously tended nails.

"This man wanted to die. I made him laugh a little. He got back on the road of life that we travel with beating hearts. Mr. Happy will be the hero of my next book. All over the world, Mr. Happy will become a symbol. Hope can be regained; the breath of life can be restored."

The lady in red leather held my hand in hers. The TV camera was pointed at me. She let go of my hand to stroke my cheek in a motherly way. Her hand was perfumed. And I, I didn't run away. The camera was devouring my image.

"Is it true that you wanted to die?" asked a

journalist, shoving her microphone under my nose.

"Well, to tell you the truth it's not that simple."

"Did you want to die—yes or no?"

I was rather uncomfortable. I've often seen politicians or businessmen flee the camera to avoid questions: they always look guilty.

"Do you still want to die?" the journalist insisted.

"And you, Mademoiselle?"

"One doesn't play games with questions of life and death, Monsieur. Let me ask you again: Did you really want to die?"

"Well, it's been scientifically proven that every person carries within himself or herself an instinct that directs him towards his end."

"You aren't answering my question, Monsieur. I'm asking: Do you want to die?"

"I'd like to die of love in your arms, Mademoiselle..."

I was surprised to hear my own words. I started when the audience's laughter rang out in my ears. This public success led me to add:

"I don't know, Mademoiselle, if one can love you enough to take one's breath away."

More bursts of laughter.

129

The journalist didn't loosen her grip.

"You've been to the edge of the abyss. Tell us what you saw."

The end of one's life is a very personal matter. Someone may have an urge to die in the same way that one wants to live... Everything comes to an end. There are times when you would like to be eternal, but eternity is very long... A short life too may seem overly long... At times you may feel that it's over. You no longer have an urge to go on. You've lived long enough. You jump off the train because it's travelling too fast or too slow. It's very hard to say. Someone may leave because he has harmed another person. We are afraid of death and we want to escape before it catches up with us. We want to escape from suffering. We leave our life the way we leave a movie, because it's not very good. Some disappear because they have wrinkles around their eyes. Because they have arthritis in their little finger. It's all very difficult. At that point, one falls silent. Those who speak are only those who have never been to the edge of that precipice where the Great Silence begins.

The journalist was persistent. She would have liked to plant her microphone among my thoughts.

the end

"There's a lot of suicide nowadays, as you know. Help us understand."

"There's nothing to understand in this world."

"Yet you want to die!"

"Do you think so?"

"By what means, Monsieur, do you intend to take your leave of us?"

"I would like to embark on a great white sailboat... But that's all a dream. Reality is heavy, heavy, like concrete."

"Thank you, Monsieur, that's all the time we have," the journalist cut in. "We can edit it down to forty-five seconds. We hope you'll be able to see yourself on screen. Don't leave before you do. It should be good."

That was how things happened, and I stayed there.

"There's going to be a lot of talk about you, Mr. Happy. Welcome back to the planet!"

I'd missed my three o'clock appointment. All this was irrational! Why had I missed it? Why had I made it? Why three o'clock? Why Wednesday? Irrational! Irrational! Was my decision to make the Great Leap without a parachute the outcome of that irrationality that was dragging me along?

Then everything happened very quickly.

Like students at a party, we fell into each other's arms and our mouths were joined. And we were in her bed. She didn't have that impatient ardour of wives who are frustrated in their marriage. The lady who was no longer wearing red leather was serene. She only wanted to play. Our bodies were very busy. I was surprised to hear her say:

"Let's stop for a while, just to savour this moment. This is good. It's like being happy. Do you know, Mr. Happy, this doesn't happen to me every day. Just think, Mr. Happy, you could have been *not* with me. You could have been nowhere."

I heard a click in the keyhole. Then knocking, the thrust of a shoulder. The door gave way with a burst of light. A camera. We'd been photographed. Without our permission. In bed. Where were the covers? My clothes? We had nothing to cover us. Two, three strangers in our room. It was impossible to hide anything.

"No! No! No!" my companion pleaded. "My ex-husband has me followed everywhere! Everywhere. But this is the worst! There are times when humour is not enough. What we need is a machine gun."

What were they going to do with the photographs? I had decided there wouldn't be any. I threw myself at the little photographer. When his accomplices had left the room he was so swollen he had trouble getting through the door. That's an exaggeration. His colleagues didn't intervene. They kept their hands clean: professionals. I had to spend a few hours at the police station. When they'd agreed to set me free, I phoned my companion in adventure. She had left the hotel "sooner than expected," they pointed out. Did I really want to see her again? As I write these lines I have to admit that I would like to see her again. It's stupid. It doesn't matter.

And so, once again, I was alone. I reconsidered my Great Decision. It was too late... The appointed hour had passed. I didn't have Melissa's Renault. I didn't feel like demolishing my Jaguar. Waste is indecent when there is so much poverty. I wanted to vanish economically. The explosion would be no more effective in a Jaguar than in a Renault. I might as well leave the Jag to my heirs. I'd forgotten to borrow Melissa's Renault. In every project we always overlook some small details. It's the same with our projects in concrete. You must accept in advance that you'll forget something. Your control is never perfect. The irrational rules through its inescapable laws.

Going back to my apartment, I felt very useless: superfluous in this life. The world would function very well without me. I had already left it. The city was running like a machine. I was an extra part. Who needed me? To whom was it important that I be there? Who was dying to hear my voice? Who was worried because I hadn't spoken to him or her for two weeks? Was there anyone I really cared about? Was there anyone for whom I'd have changed my decision? I was useless... Poor Mr. Happy!

In the days when I still knew how to take advantage of life I often wondered why I didn't have within me a joyous song, a cheerful tune, one that would have sung my joy at having inherited the privilege of life. Even at festive moments—particularly at festive moments—there was something in my chest, a sort of wound no bigger than a teardrop, a little sorrow as heavy as a pebble, a slender wound that didn't really hurt but could not be overlooked. I carried within me, almost always, some slight sorrow: a sorrow as if I had not been given life.

Back at home I write these final lines in my last will and testament. None of that matters. You've listened to the end because the notary was holding you hostage. You've often been distracted. I don't think I explained why I have chosen the Great Peace. You'll never understand and you'll soon be consoled. Do I myself understand why this teardrop in my soul has become heavy enough to topple me? Farewell.

P.S. As for my property, it is yours. I give it all to you. Divide it among yourselves equally and mathematically. I love you; my life has been beautiful. Because of that I can go now.

My dears, I would like to add a few words. Surely there is within each of us an instinct that leads us towards our own end; otherwise no one would go in that direction. Everyone would want to be eternal. Why has nature endowed us with that instinct? Creating a person only to destroy him would be contradictory and illogical, unless that instinct for destruction is a principle of metamorphosis: I am destroying you so you'll become another. When I fall into the Great Void I shall cease to be Victor Joyeux so that I can be reborn with another identity, another reality, in shadow or in light, on the other side of the Great Viaduct. My dears, you really don't want to understand now. What you want, I know, is for this to finish...

"Why did he do it? Why did he do it to us?" That question will visit your spirits many times, regularly, tenaciously. You will think that I've carried out my Grand Gesture to cause you pain.

No, I wanted to tell you that what I am doing, I am doing only to myself. It's probably not even I, but a desire within me that is pushing me towards another life. Those will be my last words.

I am sitting in my chair, quite still, with my eyes closed, just to feel the life circulating in me, in the same way that I gazed out at Mount Fuji through the window of my hotel room before I left Japan.

If life is a dance I am not joining in. If life is a performance I am sitting in the back row. If life is a meal, I'm arriving when all the food is cold. If life is a boulevard, I am lost. If life is a house, I am someone who is looking in the window. That is what I feel. A stranger come from elsewhere, I am departing now for the Great Elsewhere, where I belong.

I have accepted this thin film between life and me just as I've accepted my baldness, as I've accepted my rather mediocre stature or the curved shape of my nose. Only once did I rebel. I remember it. How could I forget? I heard words coming out of my mouth that I, Victor Joyeux, would never have dared to utter. I saw myself repeating obscene gestures I'd never have dared to make. I'm still ashamed of it but I've never felt any remorse. No one really understood me, either that evening or afterwards. My delirium horrified certain persons. I've never apologized for it. Nor will I do so on this, my last night.

It happened in Paris. I was there for negotiations about a stadium in the suburbs. We had gone for dinner: some advisers, our lawyers, our accountants, some embassy representatives, a journalist, an actress and some other ladies. I was suffering from jet lag, the long negotiating session, sleeping pills, pills to keep me awake, but above all from the wine, the good French wine that makes it impossible for anyone not to love that country. Upon leaving the restaurant, between the Place de l'Étoile and Place de la Concorde, in the rippling sea of lights that brighten the Paris night, I wove through cars that grazed me as I plunged into the avenue. Then I started to curse as only a Catholic from my province can curse. I hurled insults at Heaven. I declared that I was spitting, that I was vomiting on the sacred objects before which I had prostrated myself in my youth. Passersby turned to stare, then hurried away so they wouldn't have to listen to me. Car horns were blaring but my voice was louder than theirs. It seemed to me that the echo was repeating the words of my rebellion all over Paris. My embarrassed companions had left. Only some of the women, including the actress, slowed their pace, waited for me, not daring to flee altogether nor to listen to the lament of a sad and suffering man. That night I wanted to come out of myself, to tear the membrane that separated me from life: I saw another man emerge from myself, a man who was me and who frightened me when I think back to it… Rebellion causes the vault of Heaven to tremble: love makes you float in it.

And so I decided to go to Melissa's to borrow her Renault and bid her farewell. At that late hour, wearing round spectacles like an intellectual grandmother, she was studying. She didn't understand why I was suddenly so intent on borrowing her wheels, as she put it. I told her I was haunted by nostalgia for the first cars that I'd driven, two centuries ago when I was her age.

"There's a very strange look in your eyes, little papa. You don't look the way you usually do. Is something wrong?"

Most likely I wanted to confide my secret again, to share it rather than keep it for myself; I heard myself say:

"A very close friend wants to die…"

"Is he sick?"

"He's very well, but he wants to die."

"Why? Isn't he glad to be alive?"

"He wants to stop living."

"It takes courage to leave life when you're alive, a hell of a lot of courage. I respect him."

"He doesn't know exactly why he wants to die. He says that he's tired, that he doesn't want to travel any farther along the road: so he wants to stop, he wants to stretch out in the grass as if he were taking a nap. And he doesn't want to get up again."

"You know, little papa, a lot of people commit suicide. Especially young people. The old hang on like crabs on a rock. Is this friend of yours young? No, I know, you don't have any young friends. Only me. I hope I'm the only official representative of the contemporary era in your life! Little papa, why are you telling me about this friend? He must be a terrible pessimist: wanting to die in May... If you ask me, I think that when people want to die it's because they're bored with life."

"Let's talk about something else. You know, I've thought about you a lot. I've been seeing you in my mind..."

"Tell me about your friend. I bet he's someone who never looks sad... I've read that deep down, the most cheerful people are the saddest. They laugh to hide their sorrow."

"Ever since my friend decided not to linger in this world, he's been a little sad. He's a man who used to enjoy celebrating life."

"Why would he want to leave life, if he loves it?... And you, little papa, aren't you staying with your friend?"

"No, he needed to be alone."

"You're sad, little papa... Is it because of your friend?"

"I feel close to him."

"Do you think he's still alive right now?"

"A little."

"You can spend the night here with me, little papa. I'll wear that nightgown you like so much."

"Thank you, Melissa, but I have things to do. Let me have the keys to your Renault. I'll leave you mine to the Jaguar. Goodbye."

And I left Melissa, without taking her in my arms. If I had, I wouldn't have been able to leave. She said to me:

"See you tomorrow."

I said nothing, to avoid a lie.

I couldn't take my leave without bidding Melissa's mother farewell. You're unhappy, my dears, that I love both mother and daughter. I love all women. With Melissa, with her mother—I should say thanks to them, thanks to both of them—I can be lover, father, son. Melissa and you, her mother, you have given me the past, my vanished youth, but you've also given me a number of lives. Thank you for that. You'll never know how sincere I am. Through you I have been reborn several times.

Know that I have loved you both. I wouldn't want one of you to be wounded because I loved the other too. The pagans, who were less foolish than we are, honoured a number of gods and goddesses at once. Why must we love just one woman at a time? Can we not be fond of both white wine and red? Champagne and cognac? When we gaze at the sky must we be fascinated by just one star? Can we not like both Van Gogh and Turner? Love just one woman? Do we restrict ourselves to eating a single cheese, listening to a single song, following a single road? Love just one woman? Do we limit ourselves to living just one day? If we love the day must we detest the night? To Melissa and to you, her mother, I say thank you. I have been your son. I've been your father too. I have been your friend. Don't blame one another. Don't hurt yourselves. Only think:

That man loved us. If you have loved me a little, know that your love has been precious to me.

I was thinking about all of that as I was driving the tiny Renault. I was also thinking about my own children who are scattered far from me on this last night. Each of them free. Free to follow his or her own orbit.

The sky was hazy. Veiled. Pollution? Clouds that foretold dismal weather? The sorrow of the world? It was as if all the stars had fallen over the suburbs. (Yes, it's poetry.) And beneath the dark sky I thought: No star has appeared for my last night. I should have felt a twinge of regret at the thought that never again would I see any stars. I had no regrets. In the rear-view mirror I spied the glow of my cigarette in the darkness of the car: A little star, my little star that will be extinguished in the Great Explosion.

Perhaps the human body is itself a kind of star for beings who exist in a different place and in a different way from humans. We are perhaps merely brilliant shapes who make them wonder if we have life, intelligence, language, thought. I am a spark that will be extinguished because it has been consumed. That's what I was thinking as I made my way to Melissa's mother. And I thought: On the other side of the Great Viaduct, what is there? We have learned to think that on the other side it is darkest night that rules. Perhaps there is nothing but fire?

Dear sons and daughters, I've thought of you all. I won't see you again. And I haven't felt the need to hold you to my heart, to feel your warmth one last time.

What made me think about those busts of myself?... You remember, I know... Angelo—I haven't forgotten his name—Angelo, a sculptor in Milan, persuaded me to order a bust of myself. With my balding head and my cheeks, I had something of the look of a Roman emperor, he explained. The finished bust could be reproduced in as many copies as I wanted, and in concrete, given my concern with making concrete into a noble material. He was well informed. Angelo's father was the chairman of Milan's Subway Commission, and my associate, Robert, and I had made a submission to him. Of course I ordered several busts: one for each of the children, one for the office, some for certain ladies and some to keep in reserve. Dear children, did you think I didn't notice how embarrassed you were when you opened the crates and took out the head of your father? You stowed my Roman emperor's head in your closets, attics, garages. Sometimes my head fell from your hands and shattered like an egg. The biggest hypocrites told me:

"You're here with us, we can see you, speak to you; you're here in the flesh. So why do we need your head in concrete on the piano or the bookcase?"

That was a good reason to hide my bust in the basement, behind the furnace. My dears, now that I'm no longer with you, now that I'm no longer flesh and bone, will you keep at your sides the paternal head disguised as a Roman emperor and modelled by Angelo, son of the chairman of the Milan Subway Commission? In the end I got only a pathetic little contract from him. We had been judged—we, the champions of concrete—to be a pitiful little company. Someone else had no doubt ordered more busts from Angelo than I had.

Even if you've had enough of listening to the good notary read my will, listen to this secret. I think it's quite amusing.

At the time I hadn't yet gone into concrete. Have I told you that already? I've reached the age when people repeat themselves. It was back in the days when I was trying to be a poet. In the winter it cost a fortune to heat my house as it was assailed by the wind that whipped across the plains of Abitibi. Following the logic of so many Canadian birds, I went south to build my nest in Florida. All I could afford was the Inn Beneath the Stars. Fortunately, I was often invited to a hotel by young girls who had left their northern offices; they were in Florida for two weeks in search of a sunburn and one or two nights of love. Generally I lived on the beach. My mother's teachings were stronger than my sloth: I bathed, I shaved, I washed my clothes. I was so clean I often passed for a young businessman on holiday. I was frequently invited to a tennis match, a drink, a dinner. That was how I met a man who manufactured plastic objects. By the end of our meal we were business partners. I'm ashamed to admit that, but I feel a certain pleasure too.

I had noticed that during their brief vacations on the beaches of Florida, tourists went crazy. Released from their climate of ice, their blood boiled in the sun, they felt emancipated from all laws. Monumental friendships were forged, eternal loves were set ablaze in minutes. When vacations were over the dream ended too. What was left? As a poet I knew that the dream would remain, polished again and again by nostalgia. Aside from the dream, nothing. A memory perhaps? Memories grow dim, like a gleam of light reflected in running water.

That is why we need enduring memories. The plastics man and I soon arrived at an agreement: memories were what we would produce. We rented space in a building near the beach. "Everlasting memories, discretion guaranteed," we promised. We started making prints: nose, hand, foot, breasts, buttocks. Sometimes the souvenirs were more intimate. We hired an artist who painted portraits in seven minutes: he knew how to add colour where it was needed. Our customers left happy, taking with them an undying memory of someone they had loved for a few hours under the Florida sun.

Why have I told you that? I picture an old man opening a box of dried-up, yellowing papers and coming upon a plastic foot with red toenails—all that remained of a night when skin had baked under the Florida stars.

That was a long time ago… Why did I think of it on my way to Melissa's mother? My dears, I bequeath you that venture as well!

Why, my dears, did I want to leave you that idiotic memory, that ridiculous image? Why, at this moment, when the time remaining is too short, have I tried to leave you a smiling image of me? The memory may not even be amusing: it is tragic because it is foolish. Foolish as we are at the age when we don't know that one day life will end.

Then I had a peculiar thought. Tonight, dear children, I realized that you too will die. You are what you are in my mind. You are my memories of you. You are the questions you used to ask me. You are your dreams, which I remember. You are your growing little bodies that I see come alive upon the film of my memory. You are all those children's cuddles. You are all the dramas that caused you so much pain. You are all those adolescent rebellions. You are all those secrets so preciously kept but easily pierced by anyone who was once a child. You are the games you invented. You are all your toys. You are the despair that stifled you when it seemed as if life had stopped loving you. You are that incomprehension of the world deep in your big eyes. You are the curiosity that wanted to know the whole of that world in which you were too small. You are the first step you took, the first cry, the first word. You are that tiny thing I caressed in your mother's belly. You are that anticipation when we tried to imagine you. You are the blazing fire of your parents' love who made you, though you couldn't know in your night what was happening. You are all those nights interrupted by your tears. You are the pleasure you gave us when we watched you being what you were. You are our joy at seeing you, in turn, inventing life. You are that attempt to hold your pencil and trace letters along a line. You are the pain that was like a laceration when you left home. When I take my Great Bow, all of that will disappear. It's all those things about you that will die. I have set out on this journey to a land from which no one returns. You too will be on your way to the Great Exile.

As for me, I shall live in your memories. I remain. You are moving on. Part of your life will already be on the other side of the wall that can only be crossed in one direction. And for goodness' sake don't be sad about it! Can't you see that I'm writing these words because I'm scared, because I'm hesitating, because it seems to me that the hour has come too soon, because I want to stay with you?

Melissa's mother was surprised to see me. I usually phone her first. It's simple courtesy. An old engineer who used to travel a lot once confided to me:

"The secret of my conjugal happiness is very simple. I attribute the success of our marriage to it and nothing else. I always call my wife at least an hour before I arrive. That gives her lover time to get away. Since I always warn her that I'm on my way, she knows that I'll never surprise her. And so she doesn't suffer from the tension that undermines households in which the man comes bursting in like a ghost from another life."

How I wish I'd been given that advice earlier. It would have spared us, dear children, separations, moves, battles over houses, furniture, utensils, it would have saved us from reproaches, accusations, legal proceedings. Those persons whose love makes them suffer become wild animals. And a wounded wild animal is dangerous. Your mothers and I suffered in our love. We were wounded. And we became ferocious...

Melissa's mother told me:

"You didn't phone, kitten, you've arrived out of the blue. Did you want to surprise me? Too late! My lover escaped by the fire escape... And I haven't had time to get dressed! You aren't even smiling..."

I was already sitting in the easy chair and I'd pulled off my shoes.

"Has something happened to you?"

"No! Not yet...!"

"That look on your face, like a prisoner on

his way to the gallows, won't bring you anything good."

After a brief silence I decided to admit:

"I'm depressed."

"That's normal, kitten. Everybody's depressed. Is there any reason for you not to be? Have you met anyone recently who's not depressed? Pollution is choking the planet, unemployment, holes in the ozone layer, AIDS, politics, ethnic conflicts, nationalism, fatigue, old age that's going to catch up with you, children who carry on as if they were our parents, your bankruptcy, kitten, your bankruptcy… And you're no longer the proud rooster you once were; that's hard on a man. Don Juan is weary… Tell me, kitten, how could you be anything but depressed?"

"It's not the recession… It's not pollution… I feel like an orphan."

"You've lost your parents; now you're next in the line of fire; kitten, you know you're going to fall. You know that growing old isn't living. How could you be anything but depressed? And when all this is over you don't even know where you've come from; you don't know why you've come; you don't know why you've done what you've done. You don't understand why it all has to end.

the end

"There are some reasons to be happy… Being here is better than not being here. It's better to have the time that's left us than not to have any. It's better to live without understanding than not to live. It's better to live depressed than not to live.

"Kitten, I'm no longer a young woman. My daughter Melissa is younger and more beautiful than I am. I'm not the richest or the most amusing, but you've chosen me as your friend. Why not accept life the way you've accepted me, even if it's sometimes not as perfect as you'd like?"

"I feel as if I'm made of rubber or plastic. I don't feel anything any more. Look, when you opened the door and I saw you in your nightgown I didn't feel a thing. At another period of my life I would have vibrated like a great bell when it's struck by its clapper. Nothing excites me any more. I look at life the way a drunk who's no longer thirsty looks at an empty bottle."

"At our age, when our legs are a little stiff, we walk along a paper bridge stretched over the abyss."

"You have a strange way of restoring my appetite for life!"

"You and I can't tell one another: It doesn't matter, I'm going to begin again. At the point we've reached, we don't begin anything again…

We just go on. We hope to go on. It's a privilege to go on. So many people have fallen…"

"What you say is sad…"

"Victor, you're like a fish that would like to hop onto the beach."

"I feel more like a fish that strayed onto the sand and now is wriggling with the desire to get back into the sea."

"Think about everything that's still possible. Victor, if I'm too old for you…"

"You're much younger than I am."

"Victor, if you need a young friend, a very young friend… I'll cry, but it won't make me as sad as watching you waste away."

Just then Melissa's mother came up to me, she put her arms around me, she pressed her warm body against me, lightly, because she didn't want me to feel stifled. She said:

"To think, that we could have not lived!"

"Yes," I admitted, "I'm glad to have been here."

"It's hard, your company's collapse…"

"Yes, a life in concrete is a heavy thing."

"My poor kitten, you're so tedious. Do you want to rest? Do you want to stay with me…?"

Melissa's mother was beautiful: beautiful as women are who haven't run away from life. I said:

the end

"Thanks, but I need to be alone a little."

"When you're alone, Victor, please don't look at yourself in a mirror. You might see a stranger you don't recognize."

I left without kissing her. I didn't know why I was leaving and I didn't know why I had come.

On my way back to my place I thought that many people don't live a very interesting life, yet, in spite of everything, they go on. That's their business. Not mine. To bow to the tyranny of a monotonous life is a way of taking your life in little daily doses. That was none of my concern.

I also thought about my father. He didn't refuse to leave when the Black Ship came to fetch him.

And I, who was still there, wished that my father hadn't gone. I would have liked to be not an adult but a child. I would have liked my mother to take me in her arms and hold me close. And I thought that I had no memory of those tender embraces my mother used to give me when my sorrow was too vast—as it is tonight.

When I got back home I found these notes for my last will and testament and I decided what would be the last line of it: There is nothing except life. That's the message I wanted to leave you, my dears. And even life must have an end.

ROCH CARRIER

After that I will go and place in Melissa's Renault the cans of gasoline that I filled during the week. Oh what an ending it will be! The man of concrete will burst into flames! The man of concrete will explode like a grenade. "The pot-bellied bald little man has immolated himself," people will say. "We didn't really know him!" they will repeat.

This is the end of my last will and testament. The time has come for my final farewells. It will all be over at dawn. At that moment I shall invest my modest flame in the conflagration of the light of day.

I, Victor Joyeux, an engineer who analyses complex situations, draws up plans, balances structures, foresees the unforeseeable, I am moving forward and I am afraid. Yes, my dears, afraid. I'm afraid of death just as at certain moments I have been afraid of life. I'm afraid that I will not encounter God on the other side of life. Perhaps He is no more present on the other side than He is on this one. I am also afraid of meeting Him. If He is not on this side, perhaps He is on the other? I'm afraid of being alone with myself. Some children's stories talk about a genie enclosed in a bottle. I feel enclosed within myself. If I am taking the Great Drive, I am doing it to set myself free: to free my confined soul. And I'm afraid. I'm afraid of killing my soul. Then I would no longer exist: like all those beings whose traces have been erased by other beings, who were alive, I am afraid. If my soul isn't killed in the Great Collision, I'm afraid of finding myself face to face with it: Myself without my body, I shall be face to face with my soul and I shall be obliged to explain myself like a criminal in court. I am afraid like a child who is terrified by night and by sleep.

My dears, it's not easy to leave. I am leaving because...because I've never stayed in a place where I was bored. More than you it is myself that I am leaving. Inside me, my soul is bored. My soul wants to leave in the way that we slip out of a theatre during intermission. My soul is telling my body: "Coming with me, darling?" like the girls in certain parts of Paris.

Boredom is not perhaps a good reason to leave. If everyone did as I'm doing the cities would be emptied of their inhabitants, the streets deserted. Boredom is even more widespread than poverty. The cities are populated with people who were fleeing boredom; they have clustered together thinking that if millions of them were bored together, it would be more fun.

My life has been interesting. Often I've thought of those people who are slaves to a life they dislike. I've often thought of you, my dears. I am thinking of you at this moment: you don't all have interesting lives. I haven't shared my life with you enough. I regret that. Out of a certain sense of propriety, out of a certain respect for you who have lives in which each coming season will resemble the one from the year before, I kept to myself my secrets, my challenges, my difficulties, my joys, my successes, my failures, my discoveries... I should have shared with you... When I've left you, please don't say the word "suicide." I am threatening to come back to tell you that the person who committed suicide wasn't me, my dears, but those among you who put up with a monotonous life.

As for me, life on the other side is offering me an adventure. I know too well the life on this side of the Great Curtain. I'm like the hands of an old clock that have circled the dial too many times; I have travelled around the Earth too many times. I know that I haven't seen everything. I know that I could live another three hundred years and still not see everything on this planet. Believe me, the time has now come to disappear. I remember how excited I was when I was drawing up the plans for our first international project. I didn't eat. I didn't sleep. I didn't make love. I had stopped being on Earth. I was flying. There was neither day nor night. There was no solitude. I was coming into the world. Never had a day off school made me so happy! I was on fire as I was the first time I held in my arms a little girl who allowed me to kiss her. I was designing our bridge and I felt as if I were inventing the river. I was as powerful as the seismic shock that had thrown up the Rockies! In those days I knew where my road was. I had chosen life. I knew how I could at once seduce it and harness it. Leaving it, I'm as excited as when I arrived there with my slide rule and set squares and pencils. Ending is the only challenge, as beginning was. Farewell. I shall leave when dawn arrives.

I'm back. I slept for a while. I woke up like one awakening from a long sleep, rested. My mind is very clear. My thoughts are lucid. I am ready. The cans of gasoline are beside the car. There is gas in the tank. I have cigarettes, my keys, my driver's licence. I'm afraid. And at the same time, I'm eager. I am however a little disappointed in myself. I am leaving like a fearful man. Leaving the stage I have butterflies like a bad actor who is about to walk on. My dears, I'll make a fine explosion. Fireworks. But will anyone see it? I won't.

I feel let down as I leave. For my final day I've lacked imagination. I should have made the final day the most beautiful day of my life. I should have lived this final day like someone who has been given the right to live for just one day. I should have lived on this day everything I've been unable to live during the rest of my life. This final day is the most mediocre one of my entire history. I'm tired. This day is devoid of desire. It is a day devoid of imagination.

I should have taken advantage of this final day to see a funny movie, like *The Three Stooges Meet Hercules*. I'd have laughed again as I watched Hercules crack nuts by folding his arm over his biceps. How ironic, using modern technology to reduce Hercules, the great god of mythology, to the role of a nutcracker. I should have gone to sky-diving school and learned how to float through the sky like a leaf in the wind... I should have decided to board a train and travelled from station to station across this country that stretches between two oceans. I should have undertaken to reread *Remembrance of Things Past*. I should have gone to the race track and got into a racing car that has to be held back from leaving the ground. I should have gone to Italy and swum across that lake, as I did when I was young, through the sailboats that were taking part in a race, while my worried friends on shore wondered if I'd sunk from exhaustion. I should have gone under the bridge to talk to that university classmate who was a famous lawyer and now is rotting away, homeless, in the cold wind of the city. I should have had a little more imagination. My dears, I love you. I want you to carve these words on my tombstone: "In spite of everything he still loves life."

As for my possessions, my dears, they belong to you. Divide them up in harmony. I know that's hardly possible. Try. I'm too tired to do it myself. I don't want to be an accountant or a judge. I've written too much. I've finished now. I'm getting into the little Renault.

My dears, treat Melissa gently. Love her. Don't look down on her. She believes in reincarnation. She's told me about it with conviction. She often tried to convince this old sceptic. And maybe she's right: When everything is finished perhaps all is not finished.

When my mother took out her big box camera to preserve the historic moments of our life, she always said:

"Smile, little man, smile like someone who will go far in life."

Then I'd struggle to smile on film. I imitated the others, who smiled without being asked. When the photos were developed I wasn't smiling.

"You look so sad, little man! You seem to be carrying the world on your shoulders. Poor little man: you'll have to learn how to smile... People who are too serious have a lean time of it. Look at your father..."

I was born with a stone of sorrow in my stomach, like a gallstone. Is it heavy enough now to drag me away? What a makeshift job is human life!

the end

Comments

The engineer Victor Joyeux has passed away. I've made a few minor changes to his last will and testament but I have not betrayed his words. I've also changed a few names and numbers. That was the essential condition I had to respect. Otherwise his family wouldn't have allowed me to publish this last will and testament that I'd like to have written myself.

It came to me in the following manner. At a book fair a reader confided to me that he had an interesting text in his possession.

"How do you know that?" I asked.

"I'm a police officer," he replied with a wink.

"And you think that..."

The reader smiled.

"I'm working on an M.A. in classical literature."

Some time ago the leading newspapers announced in their obituary columns the accidental death of the engineer Victor Joyeux.

His will was found on the seat of a Renault by the police officer who is a student of classical literature. At his own expense the officer made a photocopy of it which he presented to me at the book fair. I was involved in publishing at the time.

ROCH CARRIER

With his knowledge of literature what future will this young officer have on the police force? I can't help wondering about that.

As he turned the will over to me, the future officer of literature also gave me some details about the accidental death of the engineer Victor Joyeux.

His body was found lying in a pool of gasoline from a can that had overturned near him. A cigarette had rolled beside his cheek. No doubt it was extinguished at the moment the engineer fell.

There were more than a dozen gas cans close to the site of the accident. As for the cigarette, why had it gone out? According to the investigation, Victor Joyeux didn't usually smoke. That is confirmed by his will.

According to that document there is no doubt at all that the engineer Victor Joyeux wanted to take his life at a moment of his own choosing.

Unfortunately, as the police officer told me, he encountered an obstacle along the way.

As ascertained by his last will and testament, the engineer Victor Joyeux borrowed his young lady friend's Renault. The Renault was no longer young. Oil leaked from it and formed a puddle in the parking lot. The engineer slipped.

the end

Victor Joyeux lost his footing. His head crashed against the wall of the garage, which is made of concrete. The autopsy determined that the shock had broken his cervical vertebrae.

I offer my condolences to the engineer's family. According to the police officer, Victor Joyeux has left us a literary monument "more important than everything he built in concrete."

Only the future can tell.

As for me, I believe that the finest monument still is life, where sometimes chance and reason meet and coincide.

Roch Carrier

P.S. My thanks to the grieving family. Without their respect for the art of words, this book would not have seen the light of day.